BROKEN TRUTHS

BROKEN TRUTHS

ALESSANDRO ROBECCHI

Translated from the Italian by Gregory Conti

OTHER PRESS
NEW YORK

Originally published in Italian as *Le verità spezzate* in 2024
by Rizzoli, Milan

This work was translated with a grant from the Center for Books and Reading of the Italian Ministry of Culture.

Production editor: Yvonne E. Cárdenas
Text designer: Patrice Sheridan
This book was set in Chaparral Pro by
Alpha Design & Composition of Pittsfied, NH

1 3 5 7 9 10 8 6 4 2

Library of Congress Cataloging-in-Publication Data
Names: Robecchi, Alessandro author | Conti, Gregory, 1952- translator
Title: The broken truths : a novel / Alessandro Robecchi ; translated from the Italian by Gregory Conti.
Other titles: Verità spezzate. English
Description: New York : Other Press, 2026. | "Originally published in Italian as Le verità spezzate in 2024 by Rizzoli, Milan"—Title page verso.
Identifiers: LCCN 2025038729 (print) | LCCN 2025038730 (ebook) |
ISBN 9781635425680 paperback acid-free paper |
ISBN 9781635425697 ebook
Subjects: LCGFT: Thrillers (Fiction) | Fiction | Novels
Classification: LCC PQ4918.O3 V4713 2026 (print) | LCC PQ4918.O3 (ebook)
LC record available at https://lccn.loc.gov/2025038729
LC ebook record available at https://lccn.loc.gov/2025038730

Publisher's Note

THE TRUTH NEVER SEEMS TRUE.

—GEORGES SIMENON

I

"PUT YOUR CLOTHES BACK ON."

The doctor turned his back on him, trod heavily across the six feet that separated him from his desk, and sat down, as though to compile some kind of report, but he didn't compile anything, he clasped his hands on the desktop and looked at him with a mixture of friendship and indolence, resigned.

"Well?"

"Well, nothing, as usual, the test results are a mess, you're a mess, Manlio, let's chalk it up to old age and leave it at that."

Manlio Parrini chuckled.

Carlo Dizzani, his doctor, has been his friend since time immemorial. Since they had called him in an emergency when an actor collapsed on the set, and he had arrived, a young doctor on call, fast, efficient. He'd resolved the problem, kid stuff in clinical terms, and had hung around a little to observe, enraptured by that circus of cut-and-dried orders and technically mysterious maneuvers. Lights, filters, camera right, camera left, roll camera, action! Without anyone having asked him, with one of those agreements made with glances and chin thrusts, he had become the official physician on every set directed by Manlio Parrini, the Maestro, and then confidant, friend. He'd even married an actress; that's life. And after the Maestro had stopped shooting, after the worldwide success of *Broken Truths*, Dizzani was the only animal present on those sets with whom Parrini had kept in touch.

Checkups, emergency operations, consults, every so often a dinner date.

"Just as long as you don't start in with that doctor bullshit about no smoking, no drinking, no fun of any kind."

Dizzani smirked.

"And for what? To waste my breath? I don't want to know anything, Manlio. If you tell me you smoke a pack a day, that means you smoke two, if you tell me you drink a bottle, that means you drink two. What I can tell you is this: cut everything in half, walk more, take some baby aspirin. We don't give any guarantees here, but at least I won't have you on my conscience."

Now dressed—his shirt collar not quite right, half inside and half outside the round neckline of his sweater—Manlio Parrini was sitting in the patient's chair, in front of the doctor's desk, a chair that was meant to be the scene of tears, worries, and anguish.

"Aren't you going to prescribe something for me, doctor?"

He had said it with a laugh, in the voice of an imploring old lady, one of those put-ons that you can do only to someone who's a friend and who knows you as well as he knows himself. Dizzani laughed too.

"Yeah, here's a prescription for you. Buy a house on the lake, get yourself a dog, take him out for walks, and take out a membership at the bocce club . . . How old are you, seventy-four? Seventy-five? Buck up, it won't be long now, they'll bury you in the history of cinema."

"I've already been buried there for years now," the Maestro responded, still laughing.

But then he turned serious, and almost lost in thought, added:

"I'm not so greedy, all I need is a year, Carlo, I'm thinking about making a film."

There.

He'd said it.

He'd said it without wanting to, it just slipped out, somehow. But now that he was biting his tongue, looking at the amazement on the other's face, the surprise painted in his friend's wide-open eyes, he told himself that it was just fine. His doctor was the first to know it, just as he had been the first to know, a long time ago, that he was never going to make another one. Finished. Done. Manlio Parrini was taking his leave from the set after his worldwide masterpiece.

From disgust, from fear, from...

In February of 1998 there was a cold wind blowing in Montreal. Parrini was accepting an award, one of the many. *Broken Truths* had become a milestone; *Cahiers du cinéma* had dedicated a special issue to him, festivals all over the world were fighting over who would get to have Parrini, or rather Monsieur Parrinì to speak about his art, about the neo-neo-realism that was revolutionizing European cinema. France was mad over him, Wim Wenders called him "Maestro," Hollywood was courting him in the only way it knew how: suitcases full of dollars and promises of golden statues.

He had discovered himself to have become a sort of walking cult. What nonsense.

Not long ago, Anita had up and left him, running off with an actor who was younger than her, so stupid. Maybe she couldn't deal with being the wife of a kind of monument, a champion, someone that all the film schools were putting alongside Fellini, or Antonioni, a director that students were choosing as a thesis topic. Or maybe they had already said to each other everything that a man and woman can say.

He had come to Montreal with Carlo Dizzani, his friend, and it had been there, almost on the pier, behind that big Canadian Chinatown, with the collar of his overcoat turned up and his hands thrust in his pockets, that he had said to him:

"That's it, I've had it, I'm never making another film."

His friend had made the same face he's making now, the same amazement, even if at the time there may have been some alarm that isn't visible now.

Now, instead, there is amused curiosity. He is sitting comfortably on his doctor's chair, his hands on the desktop filled with papers.

"And that's all you're going to tell me? Tell me about it, come on!"

"No, not now, it's too early. You're the first to know, but there's nothing certain, it's only an idea."

They said goodbye as usual, with detached affection, no fawning, and a few quips worthy of a couple of old gents who've seen what life has to offer.

Now he's back on the street. He decides to take a little detour; he's supposed to walk more, right? Let's pay attention to our doctors, now and again. So, he makes his way along the streets of the city center, crosses the piazza of La Scala, avoids the Gallery, and arrives in Piazza San Fedele.

It's a quarter to six, daylight is fading fast, in one of those Milanese September sunsets that aren't sunsets, just a programmed fade-out of sunlight, a bureaucratic process of dimming.

He is standing in front of the statue of Manzoni, lighting a cigarette. The old police headquarters is gone, it was in the Jesuits' palace, knocked down by the Allied bombing raids in '43. Good aim, the church was saved, the rest no. Even if the building isn't there anymore—there's another one, polished and refined—he sees Inspector De Vincenzi going in and out, imagines a porous and dense fog, thinks about where he would place the camera, what orders he would give, pretending not to give orders, to the lighting director. It's always like this when he's imagining a story, he goes to see the places that contained it, and he sees them differently than they are, sees them as he would like them to be.

He knows how to do it. It's a gift.

So, now, while the multitudes of shoppers are walking past him loaded down with shopping bags, tourists crisscrossing with rushing office workers, young girls brushing by him taking selfies, flanked by curiosity seekers with no curiosity plodding along wearily in the city of fashion, he sees something else. He sees a city with no frenzy, monumental and dark, oppressed.

"Piazza San Fedele was a bituminous lake of fog where arc lamps glowed, emanating reddish halos,"* wrote Augusto De Angelis in 1935.

* Augusto De Angelis, *Il banchiere assassinato* (Aurora, 1935), later published in English as *The Murdered Banker*.

He sees the tracking shot, the slithering of the shadows, the scant lights, a figure slipping into a doorway, Inspector De Vincenzi, a little hero without knowing it.

The beginning of the story, which is always the beginning of the end of a story.

2

THE DOG, THE HOUSE ON THE LAKE, THE BOCCE CLUB. Manlio Parrini chuckles to himself; self-deprecation is fine, but this is self-mockery, bordering on self-derision. He sits down on the enormous couch in his office, after arranging next to him a box full of documents, sheets of paper, jumbled notes. Outside it's dark, not yet pitch, the curtains on the big windows that look out onto the garden filter the little remaining light that the looming darkness permits.

This is my house on the lake, he thinks, I don't need a lake, what would I do with a lake? On the other hand, the dog would be nice.

His office—he'd always called it that—is actually the annex to a villa, with a garden all around it, like a little hunting lodge next to the manor, three floors in absurdly Gothic style, some flower beds that have seen better times, a white gravel driveway, a fountain that hasn't spouted water for centuries.

He'd rented it—though to tell the truth he never paid rent—from the owner of the villa, a merchant or a loan shark, or a property owner—he hadn't ever bothered to find out—who played at being a patron of the arts. Cavalier Guido Bastoni, filthy rich. He had invested in the production of a few films, back in the day, and later had a big piece of the action for the making of *Broken Truths*. He had nothing to do with the film industry, except to provide some capital to more expert producers, but his chest puffed out with pride for having made possible the production of that world-famous masterpiece.

And when Parrini was looking for an office, a comfortable den, the Cavalier had felt it was too good to be true that he could offer him that glass pavilion, that laboratory where the Maestro would be able to study and work. Parrini had fixed it up to a T—he had plenty of money at the time—outfitting it for work and life, even a small projection room, in a sort of basement, and then a large loft, with tables, couches, cabinets, bookshelves, some antiques, some impressive paintings, a Tadini, a beautiful Pericoli, even an old editing machine, from the days when editing was done in analog, using the actual film, crazy stuff.

The little realm of Manlio Parrini, the Maestro. It had even appeared in a magazine, smashing photographs, with some money coming in, after that, when it came in handy.

Before he died, Cavalier Bastoni had summoned him to a meeting, to propose a sale, "to keep it out of the hands of my shithead heirs," he'd said, and the annex of the villa, more than three thousand square feet, had become his property, at a cost of less than a city car, practically no more than the lawyer's fee. He still remembers that encounter, the Cavalier cordial and ceremonious, Parrini embarrassed as usual. The Cavalier had received him in his rich art collector's office. As a lighthearted jest he had shown him a poster, exquisite, from the Milano Trade Fair, an item from the 1930s, masterfully framed above a bookshelf. "Your namesake," he'd commented. And so, Manlio Parrini, the famous director, learned that there had been another Manlio Parrini, he, too, famous in his own way, almost a century before, painter, illustrator, with a sharp-angled Fascist style. They had laughed over it together, and he was taken aback with amazement. But a small amazement, innocuous, nothing compared to the surprise of becoming the owner of a country manor, but in the city, in the shining city of Milan, where those who live there consider beautiful the places of which you can say, "How glorious, it doesn't even seem that you're in Milan."

Then Anita had died, he had left the cinema behind, without slamming the door, without any explanation except the one in the famous interview in *Variety*, where he denied having any second thoughts: "It doesn't interest me anymore, it's a place with no truth."

It sounded like an obituary.

There was no longer any sense in keeping a house in the city center, a house for an old and happy couple, that is, he old and she happy, as he had hoped, after she had gone. He had sold their house, and he had retired there, in his office, where there was plenty of space and he had everything within reach: his books, his films, screens, the soft light filtering in from the garden.

With the old lady, the widow Bastoni, he had almost no contact. Nor with the villa that loomed over his garden. He could see from his big windows a fair amount of coming and going, the maids, the Peruvian jack of all trades, Carlos, who changed uniforms like some five-foot-tall Arturo Brachetti, now the chauffeur in blue, later the butler, later still a laborer. A quiet coming and going of people who came to talk business—but who knows what kind, real estate, probably—or nieces and nephews on a visit, or curriers of various kinds of favor. The old lady never went out. She was a minuscule figure, bent over from age, avaricious, people said, but who knows, people say a lot of things.

An ideal hideaway, all things considered, much better than the house at the lake and the bocce club.

The dog, on the other hand...

• • •

Now a bell is ringing. It's the intercom at the gate. Manlio Parrini gets up from the couch and pushes the button to open the gate, then he half opens the front door and sits back down, hearing the crunching sound of the gravel under the wheels of a car.

Sara De Viesti fills the entrance with her crown of red hair. She's tall, still young almost, has a feisty look about her and moves with a long, harmonious stride. He gets up from the couch and walks toward her, they embrace. No affection, no warm greetings, even though they haven't seen each other for two years.

Or maybe the affection is of the kind that they both love.

"What the fuck do you want from me, you old coot?"

"The usual," he says, "that you listen to me."

Sara De Viesti is thirty-eight and for at least fifteen years she has been the wunderkind of Italian cinema. Screenwriter, director, very underground, shunned by the market, outspoken, ornery, the best you'll hear said about her is that she's a disagreeable shithead, which is something they say about the really good ones, if you think about it. She had met the Maestro ten years ago, he on the jury of an esoteric film festival, she in the competition with a crudely militant film. He'd made her win, more out of spite for the rest of the jury, but her film was good. Since then he had followed her work, from a distance, and then he had called her a few times, when he had gotten it into his head, like now, to go back to making a film, but everything had gone belly-up, there had been arguments and fights. Afterward, when the fires died down and tempers cooled, Manlio Parrini had realized that he needed those fights, that those bitter arguments were as vital to him as bread, even more, as cigarettes.

And now there she is, a glass in hand, her legs crossed under her butt at the other end of the couch, her fiery red hair going in all directions. She's dressed with the attentive nonchalance of certain women who have nothing to demonstrate to men, nothing sophisticated, but with taste, wide-leg pants, a shirt, a lightweight sweater, open in the front, which is the only concession to a September that could have been warmer but instead is acting fickle.

"If you're asking for therapy, I charge a fee," she says.

"No, dear, not at all, we've got work to do."

Now there's a wary silence, she looks around the room through her glass and the white wine inside it; he looks at her, it's unclear if he's about to talk or waiting to get yelled at.

"Listen, old coot, the last time you made me waste six months, remember?"

"But it was a nice idea. You liked it."

"Yeah, a lot of research, a slew of pages written, and... the compliments. Shit, a film with Manlio Parrini, the film of the big comeback, the new-new-realism of the Maestro with the young screenwriter...Cannes, Venice...all bullshit, Manlio. You remember, don't you?"

He smiles. He'd known he was in for a rant, and it was a justified rant, he knew that, too. But he also knows something else, that this rant is creating the right climate. He wants her mean; he wants her hostile. She's the only person who can really tell him what she thinks, what no one else would dare say to Manlio Parrini: "Your idea is a piece of shit," and maybe he wouldn't let anyone say it, except her.

And maybe she's thinking these same exact things, because she suddenly puts down her glass, leans back against the cushions, and closes her eyes.

"I'm listening, Maestro."

He laughs. And now there he is, digging his hands into the cardboard box. He pulls out a bunch of papers, a notebook, a badly sharpened stub of a pencil, spreads it out next to himself on the couch, and starts.

"What do you know about Augusto De Angelis?"

"Practically nothing."

"Perfect."

"Give me a title so I can get an idea."

"A cold case from the 1940s."

"Oh shit. Let's hear it."

Manlio Parrini breaks into an odd smile, though she doesn't see it because her eyes are still closed. He's got her, he knows he's captured her attention. All it took was ten minutes. His little smile means a lot of things, and one of them, well hidden, says, "You've still got your charm, you old bastard."

Maybe that's what she's thinking too, but she wouldn't admit it, not even under torture.

3

EARLY MORNING, THE SUN STILL HASN'T COME UP, assuming it ever will. Behind him is the door to the jail, before him a new life, if it will really be new. The old one, he thinks, hadn't been so bad. Dense, yes. And he had thought about it often, in jail, every minute, you might say. Going over it, lining up successes and mistakes, it had been something to grab onto to fight off the hunger, the humiliation, the humidity that was eating away at his bones. He leans up against the wall, now, even if the cold seems less intense than what he had felt inside, less harsh, less malign.

Now he's out, and the others are still inside, some have given up, others are still inextricably in war, interrogated to the tune of backhand slaps across the face, or worse. In the early days, still astounded to find himself in a cage, he observed those guards and police officers as though they were characters in his books, but only to realize that scum like that couldn't have gotten into his books.

Now more than anything he wants to sit down, find a café, drink something hot that's not that horrible broth that they fed him inside. He has 121 lire and a few cents in his pocket, what he had when they'd picked him up, his clothes are all rumpled, his stomach is growling, his head is spinning with dizzy spells that suddenly come and go, he walks with the uncertain step of someone who seems drunk. Then he finds a little shop, a *latteria*, he waits until the woman busy behind the counter notices he's there.

Yes, he had measured the astronomical distance between those cops in the jail and the cops in his novels. He had thought often about his hero, Inspector De Vincenzi, so ingenious and reflective, somebody who read the French poets, who conducted his investigations of crimes and murders with the tools of human psychology, who had studied Freud and entered into the labyrinth of the minds of his characters, while inside that jail it was all body blows and shouting.

What he missed most in the cell he shared with a lowlife from Bergamo, a small-time swindler, was writing, he who had done almost nothing but write, in his life, and so he went back over in his mind certain passages from his books, certain sentences that he had fished out of who knows where in his mind, and then polished and sharpened, and put down on the page. Inspector De Vincenzi, who . . .

> was young, not yet thirty-five, and yet he felt old. [. . .] Some of his classmates at his prep school called him a poet, to poke fun at him, naturally. And he was so much a poet that he had become a police detective.*

Sure, he thinks with a frown, it had taken courage to depict, in those years, from 1935 on, in his twenty or so detective novels, a police officer who was kind, respectful, someone who used the formal second-person pronoun even to address suspects, someone so removed from that Fascist rhetoric that wanted everything dressed in rudeness and black, muscular. He had heard and read the warnings about his books: who is this intellectual who doesn't mimic the American and English detectives, who writes about crime here, in the paradise of Fascism, where crime doesn't exist?

"Intellectual," obviously, was a ferociously pejorative epithet.

And how many times had he been forced to chisel, and correct, and adapt, because the editors called him, reading him the documents they had received from the censorship office. This is better left unsaid, this upsets the moral order, this . . . walking on eggs, effacing him-

* Augusto De Angelis, *Six Women and a Book* (Edizioni Minerva, 1936).

self. He adapted, polished, cut. But his inspector remained irreducibly non-Fascist, not crude, not square-jawed. A poet . . . unbelievable.

He grimaces, because he, the playwright and writer Augusto De Angelis, is now over fifty, and he feels not old, but decrepit, a wreck. And as for poetry, well, he's just come from a place, a freezing cold cell, where there was really no poetry at all, and if he wanted a dose, a little dose, all he could do was think back on his own writing, even back to the comedies, all those comedies, because the theater had been a true love, and even to his newspaper reports of twenty years earlier, when he traveled on luxury trains, knew Paris, was a correspondent in Geneva, at the League of Nations, at peace conferences.

It seems like a century ago.

"What can I bring you?"

The woman is standing in front of him, now. She dries her hands on her apron, not exactly immaculate, if truth be told. They are chafed hands, red as cherries. On hearing his request, she laughs with contempt, but not contempt for him, contempt for everything.

"Sure, eggs, where did you come from, anyway?"

She brings what there was: a cup of disgusting coffee, chicory, and two slices of dark bread, days old probably, that he dunked to soften it up.

As much as the moment lent itself to it, he hadn't given in to self-pity, hadn't thought about himself in other times, in other clothes, with other foods in front of him, maybe even some good wine, or some delicacy from back before everything had fallen apart. On the contrary, he laughs, thinking about those little ad boxes that used to appear in the newspapers years ago, announcing his plays, or his serial stories, or his novels. And these things pop into his mind in flashes, like lightning bolts, only a bit ridiculous, as though he were thinking of the life of someone else. He remembers one of them almost by heart, December 1935:

Augusto De Angelis reveals himself in
this new novel
as a maestro in describing the environment
inhabited by his characters.
Grand hotels
Classy villas
Little cafés in the provinces
with all their characteristic "types"
a "vamp"
a crazed gambler
the manager of a gambling den
a Turkish pasha
Now, his new novel in *La Stampa della Sera**

Yes, it is a very bitter laugh. There are no "vamps" around here, just two hours ago he was locked up in a

* Announcement in *La Stampa della Sera*, December 30, 1935.

filthy cell, now he's eating stale bread and drinking dishwater, because we're in the spring of 1944, and there are no more gambling casinos, nor any grand hotels, much less any Turkish pashas. It's all gone, if you really think about it, even the refined novelist who translated from the French, and even Italy, to tell it all, the glorious Empire, there's nothing left but a handful of thugs who have taken command in Salò along with their German partners.

Even his comedies come to mind, the actresses he'd known, the theater companies, the smile of the great Dina Galli—what an actress! what a woman!—when he had staged his comedy *Pupattolina*. It was 1911, he was only twenty-three years old. He'd sent out the script just like that, on a lark, with no hope, and instead... What a life he'd had before him! Now it all seems so far away, and that life is behind him.

This brings him back to the café, if that's what we want to call that greasy spoon in Como, and to his life now. But he's out of jail. That's something.

He pays the bill and gets up, glad to be wobbling a little less than before.

4

HE WALKED UP THE STAIRS, JUST TWO FLOORS, BUT that was plenty. So, he waited a couple of minutes before ringing the bell, time to catch his breath. The secretary, a woman in her early forties, welcomed him with a trace of embarrassment, evidently his visit had been announced, his fame preceded him, in other words, and she called him "Maestro" and smiled at him before slipping back into role.

"It's an honor to meet you," she said, shaking his hand, "Signor Corrioni will see you right away, I'll let him know you're here." She whispered something into a telephone while he took a look around. A large front office, lots of light. A desk for the secretary, in perfect order, some chairs for people waiting for an appointment, photographs and posters on the walls of the most recent productions and a few blockbusters from the past. A large, framed poster that stood out in the center of the one wall, *Broken Truths*, directed by Manlio Parrini.

He smiled, above all at himself. You old peacock, he thought.

Two minutes later he was sitting in a magnificent office, all wood, cabinets, tables piled with books and files, an enormous window that looked out on the piazza, agitated and frenetic. All this, despite its being a branch office; the headquarters is in Rome, because that's where the movies are made.

Nothing had changed from the way he remembered it, or maybe yes, a more modern computer on the desk, two or three cell phones scattered around the dark wood desktop, half hidden by papers and documents, and the face of the guy sitting opposite him, younger, about forty-five, Luca Corrioni, the son of the great producer.

So, they chatted a little. About the old man, the great movies he had made, the current cinema—the platforms, the theaters that were dying out, the festivals—and he enjoyed the curiosity of that charming and just slightly graying man who had inherited an empire, more than that, a name printed in gold letters in the history of cinema. He seemed like a born-again Seventh-day Bocconi business grad, all figures and sector analyses. That was different, too.

They exhausted the formalities and memories, both glad to be done with them, and the young producer couldn't contain himself any longer.

"So? Tell me, I'm really curious!"

Manlio Parrini felt a little ill at ease. It was almost thirty years that everyone had been waiting for him to start shooting a new film, that everyone had been sending him treatments, screenplays, suggesting ideas, deploring his absence from the set: and the new film? When? Why not?

Now that he was here, he saw the situation for what it was.

In essence, he was asking for money. A beggar. Sure, he was Manlio Parrini, every producer in the country, and even outside the country, especially in France, would have signed with eyes closed to have his name on a poster, his work in the theaters, maybe even himself in person on the red carpet in Cannes, and yet he felt like someone with his hat in hand. He had to explain his idea, say what he had in mind, how he wanted to do it, maybe even why he wanted to do it. It wasn't easy. With old man Corrioni, the father of this youngster in a suit, it would have been easier: a complicit glance, a vague description, endless dinner conversations . . . now, no. Now it was different, now it was only economics and financial architecture. He was reminded of his remark about cinema, the only one that made sense, it seemed to him now: "a place with no truth."

Yet he began to speak, to explain, starting from the beginning—the story—keeping his real reasons for the end. It was a film, sure, nothing more. But it was a film by Manlio Parrini, or better, the film of his big comeback, and he wanted it to be clear, he wanted the opportunity to sparkle in the other man's eyes, wanted him to understand its value.

"It's a film about the impossibility of being free," he said.

Everything had to be metaphor, it all had to lead there, to the illusion of freedom and the ugly ending in store for all free men, even when they kept their freedom in check, contained it to exploit it only in part, reduced it to retain at least some fragments of it.

And then he found himself recounting in a few words the story of a man, someone who had lived through the 1920s and '30s, the years of his great successes, but who had also had to correct himself, control himself, censure himself, impose limits on himself. Walking the tightrope between what can be said and what cannot be said.

Manlio Parrini even turned to commonplaces and banalities. Yes, Augusto De Angelis was in many ways the father of the Italian detective story, he had invented his own style, he had sharpened his gaze at a time when sharp-eyed observation was not appreciated, wasn't well received, when the billy club seemed more effective than psychology, repression more important than justice. What was needed was law and order, disorder was not contemplated, detective stories were considered suspect, then put under the surveillance of rigorous censorship, and in the end, prohibited. And De Angelis instead argued for the wisdom of popular literature, and meanwhile he resigned himself, he adapted.

Then they arrested him.

Then they murdered him.

He did not get justice; it was an Italian cold case.

The inventor of the Italian detective story murdered as though it were a dime store murder mystery—not one of his—it made a nice story, no?

Yet—and about this Parrini went on at length—the story was not the driving force, for once. No, it was the image of that impossible freedom, that bent like a reed in the wind. That willingness to compromise that had turned out to be useless, that hadn't been enough. That is never enough.

Luca Corrioni listened in silence, occasionally jotting down little notes on a piece of paper. He made a list of his doubts, the questions to ask, a gesture of courtesy intended to demonstrate consideration, as well as the desire not to interrupt. Then, when Manlio Parrini stopped talking, he gave him an admiring look, perhaps only out of courtesy, or perhaps not.

He wasn't a jerk, he wasn't only the heir. He understood.

What the Maestro—that's what he called him, too—had in mind was a sequel to *Broken Truths*; maybe it was true that the great ones always make the same film, and he had seen in that brief account, in that brief explanation of the project to be financed, to be put on its feet, to be transformed into a film, the nucleus of Parrini's poetics. Truth doesn't exist, freedom is a convention, it expands and shrinks, depending on the historical period, on the stupidity of those in command, on the vulgarity of those who attempt to smother it and block it.

It was a contemporary film, a film about dark times.

Parrini wanted to shoot the story of a man who would have liked to be free but wasn't able to be. Who had restricted and compressed his freedom, and it hadn't worked. The story of a winner who had been defeated despite his compromises and his adaptability, a good member of the middle class, not a revolutionary, who had been overwhelmed. It had everything, yes, there was History that overwhelmed everybody, there was the spirit of the times, analogies with this current era, our era...

Magnificent, dense. But between here and actually making it...

"Certainly, a period piece...," he said, as though thinking to himself, but he wasn't thinking to himself, because that was the first line at the top of his notes.

Then he wrinkled his nose at the name of the screenwriter. Sara De Viesti was not an easy name for him to digest... Then he moved on to the things he knew all about, as though he were already mentally composing a puzzle with thousands of pieces. And the location? The studios, fine, but the exteriors? And then... did he have someone in mind? For the starring role, of course, but for the rest as well, what kind of cast was he thinking about? They would have to put together a team, certainly, think about the auditions and screen tests... but do you already have a screenplay, or do we have to start from scratch? Naturally, the Maestro has already thought about the photography and...

Manlio Parrini responded, telling himself that the worst was over, that explaining the idea is the hardest part. So, he showed himself to be open to everything, willing to collaborate, as he would have done with the old Corrioni. It was only an idea, for now, an exploratory mission. If there was interest in the project, they would go ahead, otherwise he would look elsewhere... he had requests from France, and from some other countries too. He had come there today out of regard for the company, for the name that had believed in him for *Broken Truths*, for...

He was lying.

There was no French producer, there were no patrons of the arts lined up outside his door. And he was lying about the screenplay. "Almost ready," he said, although Sara had left his house with her box full of notes just two nights ago, leaving everything up in the air, saying she was going to study the story, was going to think about it...

For now, there were only two pages of a synopsis, a rather vague treatment.

They parted with a handshake that seemed sincere.

Luca Corrioni would get down to work, would look for someone to come up with a cast, naturally all the choices would be presented to him, and then, to decide on the actors, the locations, the interiors, the exteriors . . . they would discuss everything thoroughly. They had thrown out some names, hypotheses, tossed around sensations. Parrini didn't have a team anymore, they would have to build it from scratch . . .

In other words, they were slowly approaching the idea that their chat could actually become a film. Manlio Parrini had rejected with a smile all doubts about the screenwriter, he had talked about the lighting—"The lighting is everything," he'd said—and insisted on one point: he wanted to have a young team. For a film about the impossibility of being free, you needed people who still believed in freedom.

He went back down the stairs, two hours after having climbed them, with the feeling that everything was getting underway. How, he still didn't know. With what limits. With what conditions. But he felt like he had taken a step, an important step. The film about Augusto De Angelis, the mystery writer whose death was an ugly mystery, was no longer something he'd confided to his doctor friend, nor even a freewheeling night of drinking, a night of doubts and frank talk with his friend the screenwriter. Now it was becoming a real problem, decisions to be made, stories to write, shots to frame, lights, ideas to be given form. Above all, money.

Incredible how things become real only when you start talking about money, he thought.

So, he went the long way home once again, looking at pieces of the city as though he were viewing them through strange lenses: today's scene brightly colored and frenetic, and fading into the sepia tones of the 1930s, shabby, wet, with a touch of bourgeois grandeur, but at the same time small, provincial, a regime out of an operetta, but with beatings that were real. The city surely deserved its own part in the narrative, no less than the life that was running through it.

But how to do it? How to render the infinite variations of the horizon? He looks up, the Palace of Information, planted there in Piazza Cavour like a monolith, was definitely one of the architectural monuments of the 1930s, Milan is full of them, massive, brutal. But all around it, everything has changed, there are no more young ladies with umbrellas and gentlemen sporting hats, but only hectic, hysterical traffic. People rushing, producing, making money. A modern hustle and bustle that nonetheless reminds him of the futurists Balla, Boccioni, and therefore, somehow a modernity that's already been captured. Just around the corner from there, the grand palaces of Via Manzoni hosting the shop windows of luxury, swallowing up Japanese and American tourists in sandals and Bermuda shorts with a thousand pockets. Changing a city, its shape, its face, is harder than changing its fauna. And Manlio Parrini understands that there, where he is right now, at the end of Via Turati, which back in De Angelis's time was Via Principe Umberto, all he had to do was to change the lighting, the colors of the streetcars, the shapes of the automobiles, to go eighty years back in time. But how to render that small but at the same time enormous metamorphosis? Where to put the cameras? Where to position the flow of extras behind Inspector De Vincenzi as he scurries here and there?

He hailed a taxi in Piazza Cavour and gave his home address. He texted a message to Sara. He rested his head against the seat back, trying to understand if his fatigue was due to the effort to explain his idea—the hardest thing there is—or to his age, or to the work that lay before him. He felt the coming together of two forces: the inertia of those inoperative years and the fever of a new task.

That at the moment seems enormous, gigantic, staggering.

He arrived in front of the gate of Villa Bastoni, paid the cabbie, and got out, heading down the driveway toward his annex, in the pale sunlight of four in the afternoon. And only then did he notice the unusual agitation, that inexplicable hubbub. Three cars on the white gravel paths of the garden, two of them police cars, transmitting the crackling sound of the two-way radio, a gray sedan, plus a van with POLIZIA SCIENTIFICA written on the side. The front door to Villa Bastoni was open, two officers were smoking near the outside stairway, in front of the waterless fountain.

"Where are you going?" a voice asked him, polite but firm. Behind the voice was a tall man, in civilian clothes, with the face of a cop.

"Home," he said, pointing to the office. And then, obviously, "What's going on?"

The man asked for his papers, scrutinized his identity card, and gave it back to him with a quick, efficient thrust of his hand.

"What's going on?" he repeated. He was surprised not to be annoyed, just curious. And then, seeing as the guy had no intention of responding to him:

"Am I allowed to go home, at least?"

"Go ahead, but don't go out, in a few minutes we'll come and have a little chat."

He looked out from behind the office windows. The scene was motionless, then it got animated—someone came out into the garden—then it went motionless again. At a little before five o'clock an ambulance drove in and stopped without turning off the engine. Two men in white overalls carried out a stretcher with a black bag on it. The ambulance uploaded the bundle and started off toward the gate, then outside, into the street, and then away, into the city. A few people came out of the villa, the ones in uniform got into the blue and white police cars, the van remained where it was. The tall man from before, together with a woman, headed toward the office, making the gravel in the driveway crunch. The doorbell rang almost immediately, and he opened the door, invited them in, and took a good look at them. The faces of Law and Order were pretty ordinary.

5

IT'S THE TALL GUY WITH THE COP'S FACE WHO DOES the introductions. His name is Flavio Zarli, deputy chief of police. He seems tense and worried, maybe he's just tired. He pulls out his badge even though there's no need, the situation is pretty clear. The woman is Deputy Prosecutor Chiara Sensini, a firm handshake, a little sparkle in her eye when Manlio Parrini says his name. He's used to those little sparkles, it means someone has recognized him, it's a flash that quickly disappears, that gets hidden. But not with Ms. Sensini, she's not one to hide things, she's sure of herself. Manlio Parrini knows how to spot the security that comes with power.

"The director?"

"Yes," he says.

The deputy chief doesn't know what they're talking about.

"But, please, make yourselves comfortable. Would you like some coffee?"

The cop declines politely, remains standing by the door, he says they've got to ask him a few questions, but she, on the other hand, accepts willingly, not even the time to say, "Yes, thanks, I could use some coffee," and she's already sitting on the couch, exactly where, a few nights ago, Sara De Viesti was sitting, but composed and professional, not with her legs bent and her feet under her butt. She's stone-faced and her lips are pursed, as if to emphasize that sitting down and accepting a cup of coffee doesn't shift their relationship by even as much as a millimeter; he is someone to interrogate, nothing more. Then the guy sits down, too, and there they are, their cups in front of them and a little tension in the air.

"Can you tell me what happened?"

So the man, after a glance from the woman had given him an imperceptible sign of assent, gave a sort of report, succinct but effective. Nora Vuillermoz, the widow Bastoni, age eighty-one, the old woman in the villa, had been found a cadaver—that's exactly what he said, the deputy chief, "found a cadaver," and Parrini makes a small, invisible wince—in the study in the villa, on the ground floor.

The handyman Carlos Manolo Pinzago had found the body, and run outside, scared. Not knowing what to do, he got as far as the annex, knocked and shouted desperately, he rang the doorbell repeatedly, but no one answered. This just before one o'clock. Then he went back to the villa and called 112, they had ascertained the situation, made the initial analyses, interrogated Pinzago, who was shaking like a leaf, and advised the deputy prosecutor on call, who arrived right away, on the heels of the CSI team that had gotten to work, and so now it was his turn.

"How did she die?" Parrini asked, in a mixture of shock and curiosity. A murder. In broad daylight. Right next door.

"We can't say anything about that, at the moment," the woman responded. Then she took a long look around the room, embracing all of it, appreciating, it could be said, its harmonious confusion. She let the man do the talking, however, with an attentive face that listened to every syllable, that evaluated every expression. Parrini is surprised to find her attractive. Not for her physical presence, not for her apparel, neither elegant nor casual, but for that attitude of a person attentive to nuance, intent without appearing to be so. A strong-willed woman, physically ordinary, her chestnut brown hair just touching her shoulders, someone who might not spur you to a second look if you walked by her on the street, yet, looking straight at you, shows two intelligent eyes. Eyes able to see, thinks Manlio Parrini.

Though polite and straightforward, it was a barrage, a real interrogation. Did he live there? Since when? Did he own it or was he renting? What kind of relationship did he have with the widow Bastoni? Had he noticed anything strange in the last few days, anything at all? What did he know about the widow's affairs? What kind of people had he seen coming to and from the villa?

Parrini answered all their questions without reticence. Maybe he was hoping to get a few more details in exchange, some more information. But no luck. Then they came back to him, to that afternoon, or better, to his whole day. He gave them a list of his movements, that wasn't hard. A taxi around noon, a modest lunch in a downtown bar, he'd paid by credit card, they could verify that. Then the appointment with the famous producer Luca Corrioni, two hours of chitchat, he gave them the address. Then a short walk and another taxi to come back home. Nothing complicated or adventurous, a work appointment, all easily verified. For some reason, he found himself imagining the face of Corrioni's secretary, that lovely, kind woman, when some cop came to ask: was Mr. Parrini here? What time? How long did he stay? They would have done the same with Corrioni, probably, but his face he didn't imagine, who knows why not.

Then they went back to the beginning, to the questions that earlier he'd answered quickly and telegraphically. Parrini was asked to explain his relationship with the widow, that is, something that was practically nonexistent. The idea to let him rent that sort of pavilion adjacent to the villa had come from her husband, the old Cavalier Bastoni, who had then proposed that he buy it, an opportunity not to be missed. His relationship with the widow was limited to good morning and good evening, but rarely, because the widow almost never went outside, and it was rare even to meet her in the courtyard when he went out. Carlos he saw more often. He went back and forth with the shopping, or washed and waxed an old black Mercedes. He had done some small repairs for Parrini, a window that didn't close right, or occasional errands during the pandemic, in exchange for a tip of small change, he seemed like a very nice person, but he didn't know anything more about him, if he had a family, not even if he slept in the villa, although he thought so.

All told, as an interrogation it was pretty lousy: no lies, not even the slightest intention to lie, because there really wasn't any need to. Parrini had demonstrated neither particular displeasure nor distress, at the news, only surprise, even though he was rather worried, and he said so: the old lady was an ideal neighbor, no pleasantries, no invitations, practically no contact. He was a bear and preferred it that way. The traffic of people coming and going around the villa, perhaps for the old lady's business activities, was discreet and quiet. Even with regard to expenses, they had never argued, when they had to repair and refill the driveway with gravel or do some work in the garden, which in any case didn't amount to much, nobody had ever asked him for anything.

Surveillance cameras? Alarms? Security systems?

None of that, he answered, he didn't know the situation of the villa, but there—he gestured around the room with his hands—there was nothing to rob. The woman made a smirk, that was something they already knew, but hearing him confirm it was not good news. The deputy chief, for his part, was poker-faced.

The deputy prosecutor, Chiara Sensini, stood up, pulled back the curtains from the big window, and looked out. The van of the CSI team was still there in front of the villa, and maybe that's what she wanted to check on, or maybe not, she wanted to evaluate his place of observation, his window on the courtyard, if you will.

Then the man got up, exchanged a few words with the woman, and took his leave with a few predictable phrases. "Probably we'll need to talk to you again, let us know your movements if you leave home for more than a day." He took down Parrini's cell phone number and had the air of: We won't call you into the prosecutor's office but keep in mind that's a courtesy. Sure, they would take a formal statement, sooner or later, but now they were only in the first impact stage, the initial evaluations. Then he left, he walked over to two officers who were standing by the stairs to the villa. The woman stayed there, in the living room section of the loft, without explanation and without excusing herself, letting a few minutes of silence settle in.

Then, a little incongruously, she said:

"I really loved *Broken Truths*... as everybody did, I suppose."

Manlio Parrini didn't say a word, what was there to say? Then he murmured a few words of condolence for the widow Bastoni, and added that after all the books he'd read, and films he'd made, and the even more films he had thought about making, this was the first time he had seen an investigation firsthand. It made him feel a little foolish: what was he doing? Starting into a philosophical discussion? Making small talk?

So he is surprised when she responds.

"I'm not a rookie, you know, Parrini? Yet there's always a little shock, at the beginning, just like in the detective stories, when you find the dead body. The procedures, the routine, the things to be done according to the rules are a bit of a distraction, but you still have that feeling of... injustice, I guess."

He looked at her carefully. Those words didn't change one bit the substance of the determined professional woman, intent investigator, but they did introduce a note he hadn't been expecting, as if she had confided in him some feeling of hers.

"The old woman was strangled," she said, "and not for robbery. This complicates everything, we're not looking for a thief or a crackpot. The absence of cameras makes things even more complicated and the old lady didn't have a cell phone, and even that alone is crazy..."

Then she gave him a smile that was part apology and part threat.

"Woe to you if I hear any part of this conversation anywhere else."

He laughed, and assured her that the thought had not even crossed his mind, and then he had a malicious thought, that she had read his mind.

"Now this thing is going to hit the press. A tasty tidbit, the old widow in the villa, plus the famous director who lives in the same courtyard... They'll come around to hassle you, you know that, don't you, Parrini?"

No, he didn't know that. Or rather, yes, he did, he just hadn't thought of it yet. He must have gotten a scared look on his face because she laughed:

"Welcome to the real world, Maestro."

But he was already somewhere else, following an absurd thought of his, a sort of intuition that he wasn't able to bring into focus. So he took a risk trying to put it into words but more than anything it was a thought spoken out loud.

"No surveillance cameras, no cell phone, a mysterious murder... you know..." He paused for a second, hesitating. "It seems like something out of a detective story from another era. I say that because I've been researching an old mystery writer from the 1930s, I'm... studying him, I guess you could say. And this investigation of yours without technology and no electronics reminds me of the investigations of Inspector De Vincenzi. Have you ever read anything by Augusto De Angelis?"

"No. Should I?"

He laughed again, out loud this time.

"Oh no, there's no obligation, believe me, it was just an analogy... but you know, when I get into studying something, it becomes a sort of obsession and everything ends up there, even if I don't want it to."

She looked at him more intensely. So intensely that he felt as if he were under examination. He was wearing old baggy pants, a light sweater, he hadn't shaved for three days. He must have seemed like an old man a little worse for wear, and maybe that's what he really was, after all.

Chiara Sensini got up off the couch and stretched out her hand.

"The circumstances are what they are," she said, "but anyway... I'm honored to have met the great Manlio Parrini. I'm afraid we'll be seeing each other again..."

Then she hesitated for a second, as though she were pondering an idea that had come to her just then...

"Let's make a deal, Maestro, is that all right with you?"

"I only make deals with people who call me Manlio."

"Ah, okay. Listen, Manlio . . . naturally, we're going to verify everything you've said, etc., etc., but I promise we'll bother you as little as possible if you promise to help me."

"And how?" Now he was really stunned.

"Keep your eyes open, pull back those curtains more often than you're used to, see what you can figure out, if you can, try to remember if there's anything you haven't told us, look carefully at the faces that show up, if anyone happens to show up . . . I don't know. The villa will be sealed off, obviously, we'll be coming back to do some more analyses and inspections. In other words, be my friend in this investigation, because right now it doesn't seem like we have all that much to go on."

"It's getting to be even more like a book from the thirties," he said.

She smiled and thanked him for the coffee, and maybe for something else, who knows, maybe for giving her a few minutes of diversion, for having made her the gift of changing the subject for a bit. On her way out she left a calling card with her phone number on a little stand near the door and he thought it was another thing from a different time. What an out-of-fashion object.

But she turned toward him again, as though she were pondering an intuition, as though something had popped into her mind and she was forcing herself to put aside any doubts or conventions.

"Listen, the reporters are going to be all over you, no doubt about it. Do me a favor..."

She told him what to do, but she didn't stay around to enjoy his astonished expression.

She left, said something to her deputy chief, who had slid behind the wheel of the gray sedan, and the car pulled out of the courtyard.

Now it was almost dark. The CSI van was still there in the sedan's place, men in white overalls were coming and going.

And there is Manlio Parrini, the director, the Maestro, who doesn't know what to think. That informal conversation with a deputy prosecutor is the strange thing of the day. But no, what a jerk, the strange thing of the day is the murder of the old lady. And it's not the only strange thing. The strange thing of the day is the face of Luca Corrioni as he's taking notes on his film. Or else...

He moves away from the window and goes into the kitchen. Opens a bottle of white and pours himself a good dose, this way he won't have to get up from the couch again. He wants everything that's happened to fall like dust to the ground: the murdered old lady, the prosecutor in the mood for deals and confidences, the film that is unwinding in his head, waiting for news from Sara De Viesti, who will certainly raise questions, objections, problems. Fine, that's what he needs.

But he has no intention of putting things in order, the order will come by itself.

He puts a record on the turntable, his great love Miles Davis, disorder that turns into order, just what he wants, chaos that generates harmony, everything finds its place without anyone trying to make it happen. There, that's what he's waiting for while he's not thinking about anything, only about the taste of the wine in his mouth, about that embroidering trumpet, turning around the drum set of Max Roach. Definitely the best quartet he can remember. And the crunching of the gravel under the wheels, Carlos battering his door while he's not there, and that murder with no cameras or cell phones...

> What is a murder, Your Honor, when it is not out of passion? It's a work of art!
> A perverse, delinquent work of art! And by work of art I mean a composition of the imagination, sober and concise in form, balanced in its proper constitutive elements, logical and cohesive, clear and harmonious, tense and vibrant.*

The old widow Bastoni was lying somewhere in a big black bag.

* Augusto De Angelis, *The Murdered Banker.*

6

IT'S NOT PAIN THAT COMES AND GOES, IT COMES IN waves, piercing, then it comes back even stronger, but go away, no, it never goes away, every breath is a knife wound, but you have to breathe, right?

It's hot.

Every so often they give him that blessed shot, but without a schedule, without the regularity of a therapy. "When we have some," one of the nuns had told him, and who knows why he thought they gave it to him on the sly, the painkiller, or whatever it was.

He had woken up there, at the hospital in Como, two days after.

But two days after what? He didn't remember, that is, yes, he remembered, but he doesn't know if the memories are real or things he imagined, he's in a fog.

There, however, there was no fog. He sees again the lakefront in Bellagio, near the embarcadero, where he was forcing himself to walk, it was more like dragging himself along, he was trying to get back some strength, because the jail had left some deep scars. He just wasn't well, that's all, he, tall and athletic, a handsome man, who was feeling spent, weary as an old man, and instead he was young. At fifty-six you're still young, aren't you?

He couldn't remember the punches and kicks at all, but actually, yes, something, but that was vague and foggy too. There had been an argument, started by just a few words, a mumbled insult.

It was July 2, 1944, four days after his birthday.

"So now they're even letting you go? Even the Germans are getting soft, Jesus H. Christ," some guy he'd never seen before had said, bumping into him on the lakefront.

He had answered back, some brash remark. He hated having to deal with people like that, having to mix with the dregs, they weren't of his rank. He was a writer, a journalist, an intellectual, for too long now he had seen the ignorant in command, people who understood nothing but beatings and violence. The jail had weakened him, it's true, but it had hardened him too.

So the other guy squared off and hit him. And he? He was sick and tired of bowing down, he had been through too much in jail, and he had taken a lot of hits.

Maybe he'd raised a fist. Maybe, he doesn't know exactly. And then the blows started coming, powerful, in the face, his glasses had flown off, and then when he was on the ground, the guy exploded at him with fury, kicking like a crazed horse, hitting him once, twice, three times, his hips, chest, and his back when he had curled up to protect his head.

He woke up two days later, he'd been told that by a white silhouette that hovered around his bed, Sister Evelina, the others called her, a sort of head nurse.

Sant'Anna hospital in Como.

He shares the room with five other forlorn patients, none as grave as he is.

He's not always conscious, and when it seems to him that he is, maybe he isn't completely so. A carabiniere had come, a sergeant, who had sat beside his bed.

"We got him," he'd said, "a guy from Milan, Pietro Varoni, do you know him?"

Augusto De Angelis had said no with his eyes, or maybe not even that, but the name didn't get any reaction, and that was enough for the sergeant.

"Now we'll try to get the case moving and keep him in jail. Maybe I'll come back for a statement when you're feeling better, eh!"

Sister Evelina had pretty gruffly told him to be on his way.

"Can't you see he's in bad shape?"

And he had turned and left clicking his heels, but who knows if they were really his, the whole hospital was resonating with heels and military steps, there were lots of Germans in uniform coming in and out.

Nobody had come later to take his statement, or maybe he was sleeping, and they gave up.

He had a fever, all the time, and he was spitting blood. Hours went by, days, and the fog wouldn't go away, he couldn't manage to tie the threads of his thoughts, as if anything that popped into his head were floating in white molasses. Plus the pain that was always present.

It seemed like centuries separated him from the life he'd led. The horses, the nights at the theater, the ladies in their evening gowns. And even from his life as an eccentric gentleman, his betting, yes, betting was also one of his weaknesses... and the theater, books...

When had it all started falling apart? He didn't know, there was no precise moment. Was he still blaming the theater? What a stupid idea. *The Carousel of Sins* had been his last chance, and it had left him with a bad taste in his mouth. It hadn't gone as he'd wanted, a hit would have saved him, but a fiasco sunk him. He remembered the letter he had written to Varaldo, to the Association of Writers, just two weeks before the opening in Genoa.

> This comedy will decide not only my artistic future but also my immediate financial future.*

It hadn't gone well, that was the end of that.

But he had been able to come out on the other end of his many lives and make new ones. Now it was detective fiction that was dominating the scene. Van Dine, old Conan Doyle and his Sherlock Holmes, Stevenson, Edgar Wallace...and then all those Americans throwing punches, gangsters, policemen, it was a gas, but also a new fad, and he had thrown himself into it with his usual enthusiasm. *The Police Mysteries*, of which he had been assistant editor, had been the first Italian periodical dedicated to detective stories, and then the Police Series of Minerva Press, and then again the cop story collection of Ariete Press, all newspapers and series with his name on them, somewhere or other, and with which he had started publishing his novels, which had launched his man, his creation, his Carlo De Vincenzi, a polite and cultivated alter ego, a poet police detective, imagine.

So maybe after all it's true that stupid legend that when you're on the edge of the abyss your whole life

---

* Letter from Augusto De Angelis to the president of the Association of Writers, Alessandro Varaldo, dated March 15, 1928. *The Carousel of Sins* was staged for the first time on March 30, in Genoa, with, starring in the role of Delfina, Adriana De Cristoforis. The letter is cited in Bruno Brunetti, *Augusto De Angelis: uno studio in giallo*, Edizioni Graphis, 1994.

passes before you, or maybe it's just because the pain has him nailed to the bed that he can't do anything but slip back into those disconnected memories.

Well, he had done journalism, and then he had even experimented with radio, theater had been a great love, and now the writing of detective stories... that, too, in his own way. He should be satisfied, no?

What do you mean satisfied?

Not even all that was enough, even there the clouds were getting thicker, the spaces were shrinking. The detective story wasn't appreciated, it didn't corroborate the touted spirit of the times: there was to be no crime in the enlightened Fascist era, suicide was banned, as was deviance, and vice. They didn't want the turbid, the unwholesome side of life.

And even his De Vincenzi hadn't escaped criticism, had been sneered at... in the era of the Empire and the bayonets, a cop who doesn't dish out slaps in the face is not well liked. And that's not all: his interiors were not well liked, the settings for those crimes. Upper-middle-class homes, fashion designers' ateliers, grand hotels, gambling casinos. Always morally on the edge, light and shadows, creeping darkness... that wasn't what they wanted, decidedly not.

But he kept at it... He'd adapted, rolled with the punches, made modifications, excisions, he didn't want to be an enemy of the regime, what he wanted was... nonbelligerence, that's it, to each his own. But the spaces were shrinking. The criticism was becoming menacing. The readers were there, and how! The Mondadori Detective Stories at five lire apiece sold like hotcakes, and the series of other publishers, including the ones that he himself had invented, were prospering, he felt like he was getting back on his feet, and then some as well! But he had to be careful.

He remembers that he used to collect, cutting them out of the newspapers, the most ferocious accusations, the most vulgar, from people who understood nothing, obtuse followers of orders. And the target of their attacks was always the same: the detective story, the mystery, the crime novel.

> The question is what are we waiting for to do the kind of energetic and purifying cleansing of all this ballast of wasted paper, as, for example, Japan has done with jazz music...*

They turned their sights on America, on England, on the enemy, in other words. Even Alberto Savinio had written about it, he remembers that well. Even he, who was a true intellectual, not like those two-bit newspaper hucksters on the regime's payroll...even he hadn't understood.

---

* From the article "The Deli Owner and the Crime Novel" in *Il Bargello*, July 12, 1926.

> The crime novel is essentially Anglo-Saxon. The English or American metropolis, with its sinister and densely populated ghettos like the marine abysses of blind monsters, its gangs of disciplined and militarized delinquents, its crowds as black as sewer water, the ghostly look of its architecture, offers the most favorable framework, the setting best adapted to the murder. It is hard to imagine a crime novel set inside the walls of Valenza or Mantua, Avignon or Reggio Emilia...*

He remembers very well how bad he'd felt. And maybe not, maybe not Valenza or Mantua but Milan... Wasn't it the moral and economic capital even during the years of the goose step, of the Fascist militia uniforms, and the Roman salutes? Wasn't it the international city that...

Idiots. They didn't understand anything... They didn't understand that having an Italian Maigret, who did his investigations, who thought like people think here, would be useful for them, too. Idiots!

"You mustn't be so agitated," a young nun had told him, passing by his bed. She puffed up his pillow, straightened his sheets.

And the pain... the pain...

* Alberto Savinio, "The Crime Novel" in *Ambrosiano*, August 23, 1932.

7

A SENSE OF OPPRESSION, A WEIGHT. AS THOUGH HE HAD something on his chest that's pushing him down, that keeps him from getting up. Eight twenty, extremely late, by his standards. So, Manlio Parrini forces himself, and in the end he succeeds, drags himself into the bathroom, then he starts in on preparing the moka pot and the sense of oppression fades, a few minutes go by and it's off his mind.

It's been three days since the murder of the widow Bastoni, and nothing has happened. The villa seems a little gloomier, but maybe it's just his impression, in the morning the courtyard is in the shade, there's no sunlight, the sky is hazy, that may be why, when he pushed back the curtains to look outside, it all seemed dismal and gray. What a weird September.

The newspapers had done their best to sensationalize the homicide at the villa, but less than he'd expected, apparently the investigators hadn't leaked much, Deputy Prosecutor Sensini hadn't talked to the press, except for the usual blather: "We're checking out all hypotheses" and "We're evaluating the situation." Only one paper reports a different statement, "Yes, we have some evidence, but I'm certainly not going to tell you about it," verbatim, and Manlio Parrini thought he could hear the voice, slightly ironic and a little irritated, of the deputy prosecutor. That woman appeals to him more and more.

So the press had thrown itself on the victim, but there too with some difficulty, because the widow Bastoni wasn't well-known, didn't use social media, wasn't a beautiful girl to serve up to the public, they didn't have any pictures to put on display, a real pain in the ass. All told, the fog of mystery was thick, the crime pages were all ready to dish out their macabre witches' brew, recite their "where is this all going to end ups," and spread their rhetorical goop all over Milan in prey to the underworld for days to come, until some other cadavers surfaced. But they couldn't dress their shameful salad with spicy or tear-jerking details, much less pictures of the victim on summer vacation or posing in her bikini, the victim was as old as Moses, and somewhat less interesting. There were some things, however, even things that Manlio Parrini didn't know about his next-door neighbor.

The old gent Cavalier Bastoni, who had financed films and foundations, a throwback to the millionaire patrons of the arts of yore, had left his widow a very nice estate: some seventy apartments in Milan, all of them lucrative, that is, rented, something that highly resembles a gold mine, one of those that will never be exhausted. In some remarkable neighborhoods no less: Porta Romana, Porta Venezia, an entire building—but this one an office building—in Corso Sempione. The old lady managed her holdings by herself, at most with some accountant who gave her a hand, so there were no companies or administrators to deal with, no financial statements deposited who knows where. Yet again, Manlio Parrini is surprised to find himself thinking that this is a story from the old days, but he squelches the thought, telling himself it's his fault, a product of his obsession.

A nephew, over fifty, works in London, a big cheese, they say, and it seems he's come for the funeral, which will be held when the investigators decide to give their consent, after the autopsy and all the other required procedures. He hasn't spoken with the reporters either. Here in Milan, he has an English wife from whom he's separated, and a son, so the grandnephew of the ancient victim. Then there were some details about the villa, because the "old Milan" stories are always popular: the audience that reads the crime pages in the hard-copy newspapers is elderly and nostalgic, and the city of skyscrapers isn't nearly so romantic, they prefer the twentieth century.

The villa had been inhabited by the Bastoni family for sixty years or so, practically forever. A fake Gothic monstrosity from the late nineteenth century, when that area was all farmland and a few taverns for farmworkers, while now it was an elegant streetcar suburb, quilted with residential apartment houses, so that over time the villa had become the sore thumb of the neighborhood. "It doesn't even seem like it belongs in Milan," to tell the truth, was the label given it by just one newspaper, maybe by the one that had assigned the case to an underpaid rookie reporter. Outside the villa gate, however, a patrol of two police officers had been stationed, sitting in a white car with no markings, for two days, and now they've gone, maybe they drive by once in a while, who knows.

About the famous director, about the pavilion next to the villa, the annex, not even a line, but Manlio Parrini has no illusions, they'll get there.

A real estate empire, so that's what we're talking, an income with a lot of zeros. Perhaps this explained the munificence of Cavalier Bastoni in selling him that little glass manor of his for small change. But even this doesn't make sense, Parrini thinks: the rich don't give things away because they're rich; it's the other way around.

In the meantime, he had noticed that he was pushing the curtains back from the windows on the courtyard more often than he used to do before the murder, and not to follow the advice of Ms. Sensini, but out of his own sincere curiosity. Or maybe because working, reading, riffling through the pages of books of the Italian detective stories of the 1930s, the watchful and ridiculous censorship of the regime, the plots designed by De Angelis, and the elucubrations of his detective De Vincenzi, his getting up for a minute to take a peek outside was taking the place of his most natural and obvious habitual gesture: lighting himself a cigarette and finding it between his fingers almost without noticing what he was doing. His friend Dr. Dizzani would be proud of him, even if just the thought of it makes Parrini laugh a little: a murder to quit smoking, isn't that a bit of an exaggeration?

Now he goes back to his papers and gets ready for the day. Among the emails that have come in there is one from Luca Corrioni, the man himself, not an assistant, not a secretary. It says that he is about to send him some faces, that he should take a look, although before they can talk seriously about them he wants to see at least a draft of the screenplay. It sounds like a reprimand. Wasn't it "almost ready"? And where is it?

"Faces" means some folders with pictures inside that will be delivered by some courier, or maybe a folder of files with the possible actors for the film, some rising stars, some new sensation. It's a way of telling him that he, the producer, is taking it seriously, the idea, but nothing more than that. Good news, anyway, things are rolling.

Manlio Parrini goes back to his reading, takes a few notes, relaxes with his second cup of coffee, thinks those things that old guys think: something's going to happen. And, in fact, it happens.

A few minutes before noon the doorbell rang. Strange, because to get that far, to his front door, you should have to ring the intercom at the gate, but instead... Manlio Parrini gets up, quizzical, and when he opens the door he sees standing in front of him Carlos, the handyman of Villa Bastoni. He's wearing a dark jacket over a yellow shirt, which in itself would seem rather incongruous, but short as he is, and stocky, and muscular, a cube, he really looks bizarre, someone you couldn't help but notice, that was it, with his Indigenous features and his gentle, wary smile.

When he's seated on the couch in the living room, Carlos Manolo Pinzago shuffles his hands, embarrassed and confused, as though he had prepared a speech, and repeated it to himself over and over, but now he's lost it, doesn't know where to start, things are spinning around inside his head. Parrini understands and comes to his aid. He tells him how sorry he is about the deceased lady, he's not quite sure if he can offer condolences to a person in her service, maybe yes, he asks him about that morning, if he was frightened, and if the investigators had given him a hard time; tries to put him at ease.

It's like opening a bottle of soda after shaking the bottle, because Carlos takes off and it seems as if he's never going to stop.

He had come back with the shopping, that morning, three days ago, he'd entered the villa, carried the bags into the kitchen, and then he'd gone to look for the widow to ask her if there was anything he needed to take care of, but she didn't answer. The maid wasn't there, she'd gone away for a few days, to Veneto, to visit her sick mother, to the great disappointment of the widow, and his too, because now he had to do the cleaning as well. So he had gone from room to room until he found her, in the study on the ground floor, where she usually received visitors on business, lying on her side. He called her name, and then shook her a little, until he realized that she was stone dead, already cold, with some ugly purple marks on her neck. At that point he had rushed over there, to the annex, and he had knocked and rung the bell, and maybe he had even shouted, before resigning himself to the fact that there was nobody home, then he got himself together and called the police. It was just after one o'clock, he had left home to do the shopping and some other errands around nine, he went to the store where his wife works, she washes customers' hair at a hairdresser's on Corso XXII Marzo, then he went to the supermarket. That was what he told the first police officers who got there, and then the higher-ups, and then again that woman magistrate, and again a couple of hundred more times. In the shopping bags on the kitchen table the first responders had found the sales receipt: Carlos Manolo Pinzago, the Indigenous American servant, had paid €36.52, in cash, at 12:43 on September 6. The change, €13 and something, was still on the table, because the old lady was a penny-pincher, and always counted it.

Now Manlio Parrini gets up and comes back with a glass of water, which he puts on the table, the other guy drinks down half of it in one gulp and falls silent, so neither of them says anything, even though there's a question buzzing around in the head of Manlio Parrini that he asks only with his eyes: and so? Why is he here, this metropolitan Aztec, apart from telling him how things went? What does he want from him?

Carlos doesn't even try to pretend that he doesn't understand. So he starts in again, this time with no rush and without the drumroll cadence of before. And without putting on airs, he makes two requests. The first contains all his fear and uncertainty about the future, which is no small matter. What's going to happen to him now? He had been in service to the widow for almost ten years, a job like any other, but he has no special skills. He knows how to drive, like everybody else, knows how to do little jobs, repairs, washing the car, run here and there to the post office and government offices. And now? Could it be that he—he Manlio Parrini—might need a domestic servant, somebody to help out?

For a brief golden moment, Parrini has a fleeting and vulgar thought. A butler! But he quickly comes to his senses. He's got to get over this thing about the upper-middle-class interiors of the 1930s, it's getting to be grotesque; he laughs at himself. But he answers with sincere displeasure: no, he doesn't need a . . . what to call it? A helper, a domestic, a . . . he couldn't even afford one. But he adds right away that pretty soon he might be making a film and there's always a need on the set for people who know how to do things, right now he doesn't know, but it's possible that something will come up . . . And while he's murmuring these paternalistic banalities, he realizes that for the man sitting there in front of him that's not the really pressing question, there is something else. The villa, the seals put on the doors by the deputy prosecutor's office, the fact that he, Carlos, is not allowed to go in there, where he also left some things of his own, some clothes, documents, in his room on the second floor, not much bigger than a closet, where he almost never slept but where he changed clothes like some kind of modern-day Leopoldo Fregoli, now his chauffeur's uniform, now a pair of overalls . . . It's not a real question, it's more a request for advice: what should he do? Can he go in despite the seals? Can he go in through the basement, or through the French doors in the back?

And now, there he is, Manlio Parrini, with the most amazed look on his face that he can muster, and it doesn't cost him any effort to make it, because it comes spontaneously. Go in? No, obviously not, the doors are sealed! The simplest thing is to ask the prosecutor, contact the office of the deputy and let them know... Really, what kind of a question is that?

"Signora Enrica is going to have the same problem," Carlos says now.

Yes, Enrica, the maid at the villa, half cook, half dishwasher, half housekeeper, apparently the widow tried to save on personnel.

"Her mother who was sick died the other day, Enrica called me, she's coming back after the funeral, in a few days..."

Yes, Carlos had given her the news, about the widow being strangled and the villa being sealed off, but she already knew everything, because she had been called in by the investigators, obviously. Since she had suffered a death in the family, practically at the same time as the widow, they had done her the favor of interrogating her there, just a few feet away from her deceased mother, the deputy chief of the judicial police in Padua had gone to the house, so he couldn't really tell if she was crying for her mother or for the widow she worked for in Milan. Carlos didn't know anything about the results of the interrogation, but there was still the problem of the seals: both he and the cook would have to get their things out of there, and they were owed money, and he kept mentioning certain documents of his that were in there without saying what they were—Parrini hadn't asked—and Enrica actually lived there, in the villa, she had a room on the second floor too.

Manlio Parrini had a tough time getting him to go, after recommending that he call the prosecutor's office, and that he shouldn't worry, when the cook came back they would certainly want to question her again, and that would probably be the best chance to ask... Other than that what could he do? What advice could he give poor Carlos?

All the same, he couldn't help thinking there was something strange about that visit, but he also thought that a lot of things go on around a murder, even stupid things, banal things. Practical things that never make their way into detective novels, discardable, useless details. Carlos's clothes, for example, or the personal effects of Enrica the cook, sealed off inside the scene of the crime... And he also thought, there's no sense denying it, about Inspector De Vincenzi, who hid the book he was reading under some papers on his desk so he could interrogate this or that suspect, and who, from their facial features, their expressions, their tone of voice, by studying their personality, was able to draw intuitions and paths to investigate, sniff out suspect affirmations or signs of truth.

> He, just as he believed only in the value of psychological evidence, was used to relying on inspiration...*

Not him, he couldn't do it, or perhaps reality is not a book, where sensations and evidence are artfully placed to play hide-and-seek with the reader.

He accompanied Carlos to the door while the man kept on talking. What was he going to do now? And what kind of references would he be able to present, for a new job, now that his mistress—that's the word he used, mistress—had been murdered in her sitting room? And if something does actually come up, he must let him know, by all means. And...

Manlio Parrini closed the door with more than a little relief. It wasn't like him to play the confessor, and consolation of the troubled was not exactly his line of work. On the contrary, the more they were anguished and worried, the more they got on his nerves, and in his later years he had come to accept that the only anxieties and worries that count are your own, because every

* Augusto De Angelis, *The Mystery of the Three Orchids* (Mondadori, 1942).

year that goes by is a little mosaic square of egotism that combines with the others, and it's not right to pretend that it's not true. To age is to become an asshole and so it is, but with a modicum of honesty to admit it.

Without thinking, he pushed back the curtain of the window overlooking the garden and looked out. Carlos went along, hesitantly, reluctantly, toward the door of the villa, crunching the gravel on the driveway, but he didn't climb the three steps that lead to the main entrance. Instead, he turned a corner, disappearing from view for a few seconds and reappearing after no more than two minutes on the opposite side. He had made a full circuit, but in those few seconds, evidently, nothing else. Maybe he had checked to see if there was a window left open, some hidden way in, but he certainly hadn't wasted any time. Now, still at a slow pace, he was heading toward the gate, where Parrini couldn't see him, and he left the field, defeated and disconsolate.

8

TOO MANY INTERIORS, TOO MANY INTERIORS!

Manlio Parrini is hungry, and he realizes that he cannot spend all his time in the muffled, cozy half-light of his den, reading, working while pretending not to, pushing back the curtains and looking out at the garden. What's more, he knows his working method, knows that for him to enter into the atmosphere of a film, to envision its shots, to decipher the lighting, he has to immerse himself, not merely imagine the world he wants, but get inside it. But there is a limit beyond which the whole thing becomes pathological, and now he has had enough of top hats, streetcars, frightened pretty girls with diaphanous skin. You can shoot a costume drama, sure, but living in one is... Yet he has no alternative to that total immersion, and there are moments when he even enjoys it, like when he's reading newspapers from the period, online when he's able with his meager surfing skills to track them down, or when he's leafing through the pages of the microfilm strips of the periodicals room of the Sormani library, surrounded by all those young people studying for the future, while he's studying for the past.

The language, the words, the staggering naivete, so poetic and so artificial, hearing it today. In his sessions of research and consultation he was surprised to find himself getting lost in minuscule, absurd details, especially in the advertisements.

NEUROTICS! YOU DON'T DIGEST WELL!
FIGHT CONSTIPATION WITH PILLS BY
FRERICHS-MALDIFASSI
BOTTLE OF 30 PILLS 3 LIRE.

He snickered like a little kid, he felt stupid, but he knew, deep down, that all those silly things helped create a climate in his head, a sound. He wasted a lot of time, it's true, but he needed to recover the language of those years, the rhetoric, the tone, the nuances. The same nuances that he found in De Angelis's detective stories, the old-time words.

Too many interiors!

So he puts on a jacket and goes out. The sky is a little less cloudy, but the sun is still hidden. He walks to a bar that also serves quick lunches but gives up when he sees the crowd. It's not the right time to eat something on the fly, because this is a place where everyone eats on the fly, and they want to get it done in a few minutes, they have to get back to work. Because in this area, as is often the case in Milan, there is an invisible dividing line between center and semi-center, places to work and places to sleep and live. Those who leave their desks for the lunch break walk there in small groups, there in the shadows of the beautiful apartment buildings in Corso Plebisciti, near Piazzale Susa, and those who live in the area, to avoid the crowds devouring sandwiches and salads, shift over to the side streets. The flows are invisible, unless you're right in the middle of them, because a city like this is an organism in motion, an animal, more than a place. So, he keeps on walking to a trattoria not so close to the office buildings, a neighborhood place where they know him and where he always ends up at a little table in the back, with his book, or his newspaper, to eat the daily special and drink a glass of wine.

He walks along slowly, and thinks.

He had read just about everything by Augusto De Angelis, even his theatrical works, a lot of them, too many, even though his film concerned only the last part of the writer's life, the part of the detective novels, of Inspector De Vincenzi, the censorship, of his theorizing about the genre, his coming to terms, making compromises, of the notes from his publishers asking him for more prudence, to be more adaptable, until the final tragedy. But that didn't matter to him. He had to know everything, had to understand everything, had *to be* De Angelis to write a film about him. So he had also gone looking for his earlier works, the minor ones, in order to feel the same bitter disappointments that he had felt. A man of adventure, his reporting on Libya or on conferences in Geneva, the social scene, and local crime. And then the stardust of the stage, that was his true passion, all through the 1920s, big white telephones and tragicomedies. It hadn't gone well, the hoped-for triumphs never arrived, even if the part of that world that interested him most were the surroundings, the social life, actors and actresses, the mink-stoled ladies in the audience. Which didn't always applaud, or better, almost never applauded.

He had chased down the reviews and critiques, in the newspapers of the time, and they all ended with a sort of wincing smirk... yes, but... yes, however... never a full consensus, never a convinced applause, things like this:

> The audience, which showed great appreciation for the first act, applauded three times when the curtain came down on it, applauded twice, not without

some contrast, after the second act, and once, amid some sounds of disapproval, during the third.*

All told, there were more whistles and ovations, and Manlio Parrini forced himself to find in those youthful disappointments, which were destined to continue, the mood that would later imbue the character of Inspector De Vincenzi, pessimistic and dark, sullen, not much given to the swaggering braggadocio of the regime, not even remotely akin to the New Man that the dictatorship was aiming to forge. Come off it, a Fascist-era cop that read Freud, who kept in his desk drawer at police headquarters *The Plumed Serpent* by D. H. Lawrence, and even Plato's *Eros*. So unfascistic, in other words, so unmacho and unforceful. An exception, a white fly that wanted to fly with the other flies, almost all of them black...

There, he had to render all of this in a film, had to put it in the lighting, in the faces, in the camera movements, in the dialogues... Yes, he had to look at some faces, the producer was right, but above all he needed Sara, her mean, critical eye, her crustiness... Where was that girl?

* *Corriere della Sera*, May 28, 1924, review of the comedy *Bluff* by Augusto De Angelis at the Olimpia Theater in Milan, with the Virgilio Talli theater company.

Following him as he walked along, matching his pace, was a big man, carrying a shoulder bag and wearing a light trench coat. He didn't mean to pay him any attention, but it was hard not to see him, because on the side street that led to the trattoria there were no passersby. Parrini stops, then lights a cigarette and sets off again, only to confirm that the guy behind him has stopped, too, at a distance of thirty, forty feet, and that now that he's started walking again, the other guy is moving too. As a tail, the guy is not so hot.

Now he's entered the trattoria.

"One," he says to the woman who's hustling here and there with two plates in hand. She points with her chin to the usual table in the back, his place. He likes her indifference. He likes the fact that, although they know him, consider him a regular customer, they don't kiss up to him, almost don't even say hello. So he sits down, takes off his jacket, hangs it on the back of his chair, and looks distractedly at the sheet with the day's menu. He doesn't have time to look up before a white silhouette comes into view, the man who was following him, who pulls out the chair opposite him.

"May I?"

Then, without waiting for an answer, and when he's already seated:

"Manlio Parrini? Maestro Parrini? I am truly honored," he says, holding out his right hand to shake. "Claudio Tarsi, *Corriere della Sera*, can we chat a little?"

He shakes his hand out of conditioned reflex as he thinks: so here they are.

It was obvious, he was expecting it. He reprimands himself for not having prepared some strategy, for not making a plan, for not having invented even two pat phrases to say instead of the Anglo-Saxon "No comment," which would sound a little ridiculous.

"If it's about the murder of widow Bastoni, I can tell you right away that I don't know anything, I don't intend to talk about it with anyone, and I have nothing to say."

The waitress came to take their orders. Parrini asked for a plate of cold roast beef with baked potatoes, mineral water, and a half liter of the house wine.

"The same," the other man said. He had practically invited himself to lunch.

Now Parrini took a better look at him, without pretending not to, he actually looked him up and down. An oaf, an oaf and a half, he thought.

He was a big guy, forty or so but looked older, shabbier than he had seemed looking at him out on the sidewalk. He put his bag on the floor and his elbows on the table, as though to start an argument, or a conversation.

"I know, excuse me, my work and good manners don't always go together. If it will help to excuse me, I can tell you that I am one of your admirers, but then who isn't?"

He had a smile that made your hands itch to slap him, but at the same time something old-fashioned, as though being a reporter was—and it is—a job for yesteryear. Parrini was battling with two opposite sentiments, annoyance at that theatrical intrusion, and subterranean sympathy.

"Forget the flattery, I've got nothing to tell you."

Ostentatiously, he opened the book he had brought with him, by which he meant to say: Do whatever you like, I won't be adding anything else.

But the guy, the reporter Claudio Tarsi, didn't discourage easily, that much was obvious. He went on talking, interrupting himself only when the water and wine arrived, and then started up again.

"You won't believe this, but I don't want to drag you into the middle of a homicide just because you live on the same courtyard as the victim . . . But . . . the great director, the implacable investigator of *Broken Truths* who lives almost on the scene of the crime . . . you got to admit . . . I'm interested in your opinion, Maestro, even more, I'm interested in your take on the whole thing."

"Leave me out of it."

"Yes, certainly. But I'll tell you what's going to happen. Like I found out about it, that Maestro Parrini lives next door to the villa of the strangled widow Bastoni, they're all going to find out. They'll wait for you outside your house, they'll call you, they'll put you under siege. Not me. There are things that can't be written about this murder at the villa, not yet, at least, and everyone will treat it like this, a case like any other. The prosecutor's office is all buttoned up, Sensini is someone who knows what she's doing, but in this investigation she's not... exactly free, there..."

He said a lot of things and nothing in particular, threw them out there, apparently he wanted to whet Parrini's curiosity.

"Nice try, but no cigar. I'm telling you I've got nothing to say, and that's what I also said to the deputy prosecutor, by the way."

The meat and potatoes arrived, set down on the table without a word by the woman who's serving them, who turns and goes right away.

"Let me propose a deal," the big man said, biting into a piece of bread.

Parrini shot him a glance that was meant to convey some precise things: I don't make deals with anyone, you are not in a position to make deals and alliances, your proposals don't interest me. But perhaps in his gaze there was a spark of curiosity, because the other guy just went ahead as though nothing had changed, as though he hadn't even raised his eyes off his plate.

"I won't bother you and I won't ask you a thing, Maestro. The deal will be that when you're ready, when it's the right moment, you'll let me have an interview... the famous director who happened to find himself next to a crime, something like that..."

Parrini is about to laugh, what kind of a deal is that supposed to be?

"In exchange, I'll tell you something you don't know, for example, who the widow Bastoni really was, or why the prosecutor's office has their hands tied..."

Now, against his will, Parrini really does have a question mark in his eyes. Sensini doesn't seem to him to be someone who can be maneuvered, and why would she be? The wealthy widow strangled to death, okay, it's a nice case for the newspapers to make into whipped cream, but what's with all these allusions?

"So you really are interested," Claudio Tarsi smiled. And started talking, and he started listening, slowing down against his will the pace of his lunch.

The case was a bit thorny, the other guy said, for several reasons. The first, that no one has said and no one has written, is that the murdered woman is in some way related to a big cheese. The nephew, the son of the sister of Cavalier Bastoni, is an important bureaucrat connected to finance and politics whom the government sends around Europe to take care of troublesome situations, with a role at the European Central Bank and the reputation of someone who solves problems, a superpowered lobbyist.

"He's moving seas and mountains, with the minister, with the chief prosecutor, so that this family relationship doesn't get out, or that it gets talked about too much."

Now Parrini stops trying to hide his curiosity, this Tarsi is a gold mine. And in fact the man goes on, chomping awkwardly on his food and talking with his mouth full.

He says there's nothing wrong with being a relative of a woman who dies, even in the way she did, that's obvious, if it weren't that the business dealings of the widow Bastoni are not exactly on the up-and-up, that's it, and there are rumors that her real estate empire is managed pretty loosely, lots of payments in cash, off the books, very low taxes, and maybe even loan sharking, things that come to light when there's a lot of money that's not officially recorded anywhere.

This Tarsi is a good storyteller, Parrini thinks, as he listens without saying anything. He tries to keep his interest from showing too much, but he's not convinced that it's working. He keeps eating slowly, chewing thoroughly, sipping his wine calmly, a lot different from the way he usually eats, alone, when it seems as if he's in a hurry to go back home.

"Plus," the other goes on, "there's the fact that the investigation is very problematic."

Well, yes, this he knew, no video cameras, not even a cell phone used by the victim, Sensini had told him as much…

"Did she also tell you about the evidence that doesn't add up? Did she tell you about the strands of blond hair, woman's hair, found on the dead body? And about the coffee cups set out on the desk in the office where the old lady was killed?"

"But how is it that you know…"

"It's my job to know things, Maestro."

"I haven't read them in the newspaper, though."

"I told you, there are things that can't be written."

"And why are you telling me?"

"For our agreement, no?"

"We don't have any agreement, get that into your head."

However, just at that moment, his mind turned to the request Sensini had made of him. Not exactly a request, but anyway…

"The only thing that I saw that was strange and that surprised me…"

The other guy tensed with attention, his eyes were now two thin lines, a cat looking at the canary perched on the windowsill.

"Well, they haven't taken anything out of there, from the villa. They've searched it, I'm sure, that is, I believe, but they didn't come out of there with boxes and envelopes, all they did was seal it shut."

But then he added immediately, as though to explain that his observation was somehow unreliable, "But, I don't know anything about this kind of stuff, anyway, and to tell the truth, it doesn't interest me very much."

As if to say: enough, discussion over, I've got nothing to say and nothing is what I'm going to say.

The other guy smiled with his slap-hungry face, and he got up, grabbed his bag, and put his trench coat back on.

"I'll let you eat, please pardon the intrusion. It's a bastard profession, you know? I'm sure we'll talk again, but remember our agreement. Parrini's version, the Maestro who sees the crime up close... The broken truths, but this time in your own backyard, right in front of your nose... Have a good day, Maestro."

"We don't have any agreement," Parrini repeated, this time raising his voice a little, but the other guy had already set off and was in the middle of the room, then on the other side of the restaurant counter.

So, in a bad mood, Parrini finished his lunch, drinking more than the half liter he had ordered, asked for a cup of coffee, and headed for the door.

"The gentleman already paid," the woman at the counter told him, and this made his mood even worse.

When he got to the gate of the house, having walked in reverse the short distance he'd traveled earlier, there were two guys standing there waiting for him. One young guy looking bored and the other older, on the phone, who finished the conversation just as he came around the corner. They didn't even introduce themselves, just barked something.

"Maestro Parrini, how well did you know the widow Bastoni?" the young guy.

"Can we talk for a minute?" the other one.

He doesn't answer, he's not listening, he feels in his pocket for the key to the little iron gate and sticks it in the lock while the two of them throw more questions like punches:

"Were you in the house at the time of the murder?"

"Can you tell us what you saw?"

The damned key doesn't turn right away, seems like it's jammed, and just at that moment a taxi drives up. Here comes someone else, Parrini thinks, and instead out of the taxi comes Sara De Viesti, a mass of red hair swaying in the puff of wind that accompanies her, not much, but enough to show that that's not just any head of hair. She bends down to pay the fare with her phone and then she's next to him on the sidewalk, in front of the gate that has finally opened.

"The Maestro has nothing to say," she hisses in an ice-cold voice.

"Just a couple of questions..." the other two insist.

"When Maestro Parrini wants to issue a statement, he'll do so by way of his press office, have a good day."

Which is like saying, That's the end of it and so long, by now he's inside, his feet on the gravel of the courtyard, and she's still at the gate, but coming right behind him.

"And who's in charge of his press office?" the young guy asks, now turned aggressive.

"My ass," says Sara De Viesti, as coldly as before, which brings the discussion to a close just as the little door of the gate closes with a metallic click, the two of them in, and the two ballbusters out.

They cross the courtyard and go into the house, not even a minute later and she's already on the couch, in her usual position. Only now he sees that she has a big bag full of stuff, like a gym bag, that she drops down heavily on the carpet in front of the couch.

"Thanks, but I could have handled them myself," he says.

"Yeah, sure, I don't doubt it."

"I'm warning you that I don't want to talk about this affair."

She puts her hands around her neck, as though miming a strangulation, and sticks out her tongue. Then she laughs: "What affair?"

"What a bitch. Where have you been? It's a week now that you disappeared."

"I've been studying up, doing my homework, I did some research. Aren't we supposed to be working on your Augusto De Angelis? Don't we have to write a screenplay? Or have you changed your mind?"

"Changed my mind? Not at all! Just the opposite!"

"Good, now I'm going to make you change it."

Then, without even giving him the time to figure out what she means, to ask, to decipher, she adds:

"There is no cold case, Manlio. Everything is crystal clear, the courts have had their say, and the investigations too, the De Angelis case is as closed as closed can be, there is no story, no romance."

She opened the zipper of her bag sitting on the floor and stuck her hands in it, pulling out three colored folders full of papers.

9

DAYTIME, THE LIGHT IS BURNING HIS EYES. IT'S COMING in through a large window, and it wounds him.

How many days has he been here? Five? Six? He has lost his sense of time. He asks, no one responds. He has learned to understand things with his ears, just by listening. He sifts through the noises, sounds, words, what happens around him, tries to detach the moans of his roommates, and also his own, from the general noise, from the background mix. Heels, those he hears well. The hospital is rife with Germans, with martial footsteps, barked orders. From what he understands, from what he knew before the beating and his hospitalization, things don't look so good for the Nazis. The area around Como is an indistinct battlefront, the guerrilla bands of the Resistance are giving them a hard time, the local territory is arduous for those who don't know it, a land of traps, ambushes, men hanging from tree limbs with a sign around their necks: BANDITEN.

At Sant'Anna hospital, they pass between the beds, searching for patients with suspicious wounds, from gunshots, intimidating the doctors, only Sister Evelina keeps them at bay with her eagle shrieks. One of them bent over him, too, but then left without saying a thing. Or did he dream it?

He is delirious most of the time. In prison, pneumonia killed them off in bunches, not a day went by without the cry rising from some cell: "Jailer! We've got a dead body here!"

Was he to consider himself lucky to be in a hospital bed? What luck, eh!

Everything is intertwined, all mixed up.

But what he feels—in addition to the pain, in addition to the feeling of oppression with every breath—is a sense of disaster. His rebirths, his restarts, his reinvention of a new life each time had been of no use. The tragic curve of the regime seemed to him inevitably intertwined with his own, he vaguely sensed that he was falling off a cliff together with the history of Italy, down to the bottom. And who wasn't falling? He couldn't say that he had ever believed all that much in that spectacle of bellicose and racist rhetoric, but lived with it, yes. First the newspapers, and then the theater, and then what had seemed to him a new life, a new spring. The novels, the series, the short stories. It had seemed to him a refuge, at first, a kind of port to dock in, a source of income, not excessive but sufficient, as long as you write, write, write.

And then over time, with the refinement of his character, of his commissioner De Vincenzi, he had also developed a theory of his own. The foreign thriller was liked by the public, but not by the Ministry, the prevalence of foreign authors, mostly English and American, was not appreciated. And he was thinking of an Italian detective story, of something that had roots here, that took its cue from the lives that its readers lived. Its readers here, not the ones on the banks of the Thames or the Hudson.

> I will tell you only that I wanted and want to make an *Italian* detective novel.
> Arduous task.
> We lack everything, in real life, to be able to devise an American or English style detective novel. There are no *detectives*, there are no *policemen*, there are no *gangsters*, there aren't even, poor us!, any fragile heirs and old men empowered by money and intrigue willing to get themselves killed.
> We do not lack, unfortunately, murders. There is no shortage of tragedies.
> [. . .]

> This much is certain, in any case. That if the detective novel is to be born in Italy too, it must be an Italian novel, characteristically ours, luminously ours.*

How strange, though. In that state of half-sleep and pain—with that stabbing knife he feels in his chest with every breath—he seems to remember everything about that lecture of his.

His poetic manifesto. His vindication. Was that what had lost him?

Was that what had condemned him?

But no, he couldn't say that there had been some specific act. He simply hadn't obeyed, he simply hadn't played along. A little, yes, of course. The murderers in his stories were almost always foreigners, and never, under any circumstances, managed to escape justice. But to be honest, he hadn't followed the rules, he had strayed, he had, so to speak, extricated himself. It was Milan, his setting, a lictorian city, from where it all started, in 1919. He had even shown sympathy for the

* Augusto De Angelis's "Lecture on the Detective Story," written between the end of 1939 and the beginning of 1940, appears in an abridged form in De Angelis's preface to his novel *The Seven Double Spades* (Romantica Mondiale Sonzogno, 1940). The complete version was published, edited by Oreste del Buono, in *La Lettura* of March 1980, with the title "Lecture on the Detective Story (in Dark Times)."

Jews—gone that far—and used dialect in some dialogues, something strictly forbidden.*

Was that it? Maybe. It hadn't helped, that's for sure. But the better part of it was other things, it lay elsewhere, and was so widespread and capillary, in his novels, that he could not have corrected it with a stroke of the pen, by eliminating just a few paragraphs. The environment of his detective stories, the milieu, the frame, was always that fat and satisfied bourgeoisie that went from the fashion shows to concerts at La Scala. Fascist Italy, the Great Proletariat, could only be seen in backlight, and the upper class was always at the center of the scene. Crime was therefore not a matter of desperate people, of distraught down-and-outers Lombrosianly predisposed to crime, but of gentlemen and robber barons, the rich who were perhaps grateful and devoted to the regime. His "Italian detective story" showed that there is no bulwark against crime, that it is not a question of social status, or class, or deviance, that no environment is safe from tragedy.

> Each of us, today, can be a murderer or a murder victim.†

* In *The Seven-Flame Chandelier* (Edizioni Minerva, 1936) De Angelis shows a certain sympathy for the Jewish question, and uses words in the Veneto dialect, violating the strict rules of the regime against the use of dialect.

† Augusto De Angelis, "Lecture on the Detective Story."

There was plenty to make him be seen as a dissident, a maverick. But it was more than that: the circle tightened around him. He couldn't get out of his head the phone call from Augusto Foà, his friend, his agent, the founder of the International Literary Agency, the one who had brought Italian readers innumerable talents, words, pages, from Conan Doyle to Kipling, to Simenon. It was he who procured him contracts, who placed his novels, who had negotiated with Mondadori for this now well-known Italian novelist, De Angelis, who had brought him to the Mondadori Detective Stories, the parent company, the battleship of the book, even if for a few thousand lire per novel.

He remembers how he held back his tears, how he said to him in a gloomy voice: "All this can no longer be, my friend," because the racial laws did not allow Foà to head a company. The injustices became enormous, unbearable. The noose tightened. He continued to write his detective stories, increasingly squeezed between absurd rules, censorings announced in short messages in the mail: "There would be some corrections to be made, you know, for the sake of prudence..."

He heard some words flying around his bed.

"Not much hope," said a male voice. Maybe a doctor. And then a nun who was murmuring a prayer. Were they talking about him? Was it over, then?

• • •

Even thinking it was over was a mistake. But didn't everyone think so? After July 25, with the Duce prisoner, the end had seemed imminent, it was almost done, it seemed you could hear the sigh of relief of an entire nation. He had even returned to journalism, incredible, to the *Gazzetta del Popolo* in Turin, where there was a new director—a new outlook, new men—who had called him. It was useless to look for his name, he was, as they said, "the machine," received correspondence, edited articles, did the page layout. A prudent newspaper, of a country still at war, but where people read things that were unthinkable only a few days before. He still remembers the first editorial of the new editor, Tullio Giordana, published on July 29, and how he had read it to the assembled editors, and he remembers the emotion that had overwhelmed them all, on a sultry and feverish Turin afternoon.

> Freedom is like the air we breathe, an element of the air. Yes, you can breathe without it, but it hurts and in the long run you suffocate yourself. [. . .] That's why when I picked up the pen I found myself talking about freedom. Because it is enough to mention this word to signal a platform. Deep down, that is what is essential.*

* Editorial introducing the new editor of the *Gazzetta del Popolo*, Tullio Giordana (1877–1950), appears on the front page on July 29, 1943. A

Freedom. It had seemed to him a new word, not empty like the words of those absurd and ferocious twenty years. Freedom—he had thought with a little shame—could mean many things, even writing detective stories that would not run into the ire of some obtuse censor. Paradoxical as it may seem, freedom could also mean a murderer named Brambilla, or Rossi, not necessarily O'Riley, or Smith.

How could he have deluded himself like this? How could they, who were intellectuals, educated, old foxes ensconced in the newspapers, camouflaged waiting for better times, fall for it, in that way, up to their knees?

There had been days, months, of feverish oscillation between optimism and tragedy. Now he remembers the morning of August 14, with the news arriving frantically and the front page of the *Corriere della Sera*, which he dutifully leafed through every day:

NEW BOMBING RAID
"VERY HEAVY" ON MILAN
The Duomo and the Gallery damaged—entire streets demolished
Clinics, museums, and works of art hit or set on fire*

---

volunteer in Ethiopia and in the Second World War, starting in May 1944 he joined the Resistance in Val Chisone entering the autonomous Val Chisone brigade. His combat moniker was Delfino.

* *Corriere della Sera*, August 14, 1943.

Oh, it was certainly not the first Allied bombing, but this time the British Bomber Command had done a massive job: 504 planes, 321 Lancasters and 183 Halifaxes, 2,000 tons of bombs, 380,000 incendiary fragments. He, at his desk in Turin, with the telephone next to him, and the telegraphist who came and went in a rush, evaluated and read the news. And so he had learned that the police headquarters, his police headquarters, in Piazza San Fedele, the bare and gloomy office of his commissioner De Vincenzi, the den of his poet policeman, was no longer there. It was a blow—a trifle in that tragedy of the people of Milan bombed from above—that had hurt him. Fascism had hindered and followed him, harassed and censored him, and now the war was sweeping away his places, his streets, the familiar horizons in which he had made his characters move, the Gallery, the Duomo, Palazzo Marino. And the police headquarters in Piazza San Fedele.

> All of Milan has been torn apart, has felt the fury of the enemy on its homes and offices, its palaces, its churches. [. . .] Even the building next to the church of San Fedele and watched over by the monument to Manzoni, was scarred by fire.*

* *Corriere della Sera*, August 14, 1943.

Of all the offenses of those years, that barbarity from the sky—a bombardment of civilians, no more and no less—had seemed to him the most serious, because it touched places that he had walked through a thousand times and that for this reason he had made his commissioner walk through, his policemen so indisposed to violence and to Fascism, his murdered bankers, the lightly veiled young ladies, the well-dressed scoundrels, and high society upset by his invented crimes.

It is true, his Milan stopped at the ramparts, at the inner ring of the Navigli canals, those were times when the suburbs were simply called countryside. It was a Milan, his Milan—his and his commissioner's—always composed and elegant, which allowed itself a few sparkles of a European capital, a little Vienna, a little Paris, in the small gatherings outside La Scala, on the right evenings, or in the lights of the Gallery, the city's living room, where one went to see and to be seen. But it gave the best of itself in the shops, in the courtyards, in the indefatigable hustle, in the faces of the waiters with napkins on their arms making small bows to their customers. How he loved that city, he who was not born there, its fabric of humanity, so unpredictable that the cooper could, on the streets, cross paths with the countess. And now...

A wound, that's it. No less painful than the one he feels in his chest every time he breathes.

How could they have believed it was over?

In fact, it wasn't over at all. September 8 was perhaps good news, but only below the Gothic Line. Not in Milan. Not in Turin. At the offices of the *Gazzetta del Popolo* it only took them a few days to get things back in order. The newspaper went right back to being a megaphone of the regime, those who had taken it over in those interim few months left, or were kicked out, or even had to disappear, go into hiding, try to figure out what they were going to live on from then on.

He, Augusto De Angelis, the novelist, had quickly moved on, he didn't know if they would come looking for him, but better to disappear. The Florence affair, that ugly event, happened later, when he was wandering around not knowing where to take refuge.

But now all these events are superimposed, intertwined, all mixed up. Now all he feels is that the light has dimmed, the sun no longer hurts his eyes. Sister Evelina has come over to him with a syringe and given him that blessed injection that gives him a little respite.

Another day has gone by. How many does he have left?

10

NOW THEY GET DOWN TO WORK.

The folders that Sara De Viesti has extracted from her bag, which, who knows, perhaps also contains other treasures, are full of papers, her research. In a week she had collected more material than he had done in several months. But that was as it should be. He, the Maestro, had other things to think about. The light, the angle to be given to that bizarre and skewed story, the depth of the characters, and above all, of the character. What did they want to make of it? The intention was obvious: it was not so much the story of Augusto De Angelis, which would move everything, but his essence as a free man, aspiring to be free, in a context that did not consent to freedom, did not tolerate it, could not allow it to anyone. He had tried to explain it to her, and Sara De Viesti had started to listen: however complicated, Parrini said heatedly, that was the first step. The climate, the environment, the air all around.

"We are not talking about the Resistance and partisan Johnny, Sara. We are talking about an upper-class bourgeois, a cultured person, perhaps a dandy, an eccentric who reads foreign books, who bets on horses, who writes theater pieces. Not an open opponent of the regime, but someone who is crushed by the regime all the same, remains in the midst of it, lets himself be crushed."

Yes, that was clear. And as he spoke, she extracted from her folders the supporting documents, the evidence, the highlights, almost always documents of the time.

Now, Manlio Parrini felt good. There wasn't anything around anymore to bother him, he wasn't thinking anymore about the strangled old lady, nor about the annoying crime-hound reporters stationed outside the green gate. There was only that dense back-and-forth, that putting together sensations, documents, discoveries from old books that made them bounce in their chairs, as when, putting together a difficult puzzle, you find the right piece. No one shouted Hurrah!, but they might have.

There was no script yet, no, but Sara had come up with a precise synopsis that could become one soon. About twenty pages: that they would start from, that they could go to, through whose narrow paths, or curves, they would have to pass. From the popular novel, the detective story, a "streetcar novel" as some called it at the time, which seemed like a free space, of leisure, to how that free space had shrunk. And he, De Angelis, who swam in the midst of it, partly making concessions, partly claiming his diversity, an innovator of sorts, almost subversive, but also willing to compromise, to give way to the dictates of the current ideology, if this could help him survive, allow him to do what he knew how to do, that is, write, tell stories.

He wonders if he could somehow fall in love with that young woman, who understands on the fly, who follows him when he explains subtle nuances in the personality of the character he wants to construct. But that's silly. She could be his daughter, first of all, and then, fall in love, what does that mean? They are constructing a story, together, they are reconstructing a life, even if they know it will not be a biography. Can it be called falling in love, this journeying together perfectly aligned, this immediate mutual understanding?

It seems more like synchronized swimming, Parrini thinks, or the Miles Davis quartet.

They digress, cross over borders and recross them, they're having fun. The atmosphere that the film must have is slowly coming together. Sara laughingly reads to him a few sentences, some gems of that oppressive and ridiculous regime within which their story moves, the "light" that Manlio Parrini speaks of, the one that must contain everything, that must radiate from every scene. The press releases from the Ministry of Popular Culture, the hilarious and threatening prose that came out of there, the stuff that all the De Angelises in De Angelis's time had to put up with, stacking up disgust and hidden laughter, head shakes, commiseration, but also fearing the worst.

Who said that the ridiculous can't be dangerous?

He got up to make coffee, she followed him with a big book in her hand, reading, picking flowers from the manual of fascist idiocy.

"Listen here!" she said. "It must be remembered that thefts are part of the crime news, which must be very limited and published without any emphasis."

He put water in the moka.

"Ah! And here!" She was laughing. "Ignore France. Don't write anything about this country. Criticize, however, always and in any case England. Don't take at face value anything that comes from that country."

He was putting in the coffee powder.

"No brief notes, much less full-blown condemnations, against women without stockings."

Then she burst out laughing, a *fou rire* out of control.

"Listen to this!" she declaimed, pronouncing her words distinctly, drowning out the gurgling of the rising coffee.

"Stop writing about Josephine Baker, even if it is to deplore the fact that others have been writing about her."

Masterpiece. The censorship even censored overzealous censors. Manlio Parrini laughed too. "That's what we need!" he said.

He meant the idiocy of power. What did it mean to write in those times? Write anything. It was like walking on eggshells, and so it came to him spontaneously:

"Who cares about Augusto De Angelis, what we're talking about here is today, about us!"

Naturally, they had considered the sets.

Parrini imagined them ornate, opulent. Bourgeois interiors with clocks and shiny furniture, and then the lobbies of the grand hotels, the gaming rooms of the casinos, the fashion houses, in sharp contrast with the exteriors, on the other hand, dark and foggy, a dark and murky Milan.

There, with that light, with that dim light, is where he would make his De Angelis move, in an eternal rushing around between publishing houses, editorial board meetings, appointments. He sees him walking in the streets that today are a hymn to the opulence of the market, and that then were only downtown streets, with no traffic lights, with trams and cars competing for a space crowded with pedestrians. The narrow streets behind Piazza della Scala, the ones that led to the police headquarters in Piazza San Fedele, were a labyrinth of public housing and shops with a single light. He sees him stop in front of the windows of the bookshop, the Hoepli, on Via Berchet since 1935, because before that maybe it was in the De Cristoforis gallery, who knows, check to see if one of his books could be seen on the shelves, to reassure him, satisfy the modest vanity of a writer. And then up, along Viale Littorio, to the square under eternal construction.

The coffee table in front of the sofa is a pile of books, papers, half-open volumes set down with their pages folded to mark them, or spread open, bundles of photocopies of newspapers from the thirties and forties. A treasure.

Manlio Parrini looks for a book and opens it to the first page. Reads.

> The rain was coming down in long strings, which in the glare of the lights looked silver. The diffuse, smoky fog prickled his face with its needles.*

Inside, the lights, the glimmers, the luxuries, decadent and satiated, and outside, instead, darkness and smog. That's what he wanted! The director of photography would be a crucial choice. And the costumes, too, of course.

* Augusto De Angelis, *The Hotel of the Three Roses* (I Libri Gialli Mondadori, n. 148, 1936).

• • •

But what was most urgent was the overall design, not yet the weft or the embroidery, but the material to be chosen, the color, the thickness of the fabric. Manlio Parrini knew what the real problem was: to narrate a life, and therefore to respect it, as much as possible, but also to give it the curvature of a universal lesson, of metaphor, of the general sense not so much of that life, but of all lives, of our lives. That was what had made *Broken Truths* a masterpiece, and that was what he wanted to do again.

A very delicate balance that his hand, his mastery, had to make evident.

Sara De Viesti understood this well, and she was following him into that minefield.

She reached down to put her hands on one of her folders, as of yet unopened, and on whose cover was written in marker: COMPROMISES.

It was perhaps the heart of her research, and one of the lights that, in the illumination of the story in the "light" that Parrini was looking for, had to be present.

Augusto De Angelis had, so to speak, muddled through. The theater had not given him what he expected, even if he had fished among the divas of the moment, in the pockets of the regime. Adriana De Cristoforis of *The Carousel of Sins* was famous for a silent film released in 1923, to celebrate the first anniversary of the march on Rome, a big-budget snoozer loaded down with rhetoric and propaganda, but that meant nothing. More interesting were two books by De Angelis, from 1936, *Hitler and the Rhine* and *Intelligence Service: The Forge of British Espionage*, both published by the publishing house La Prora. Journalistic works, not apologies for the regime, but all in all... They were almost programmatic works, almost notices hanging on his bulletin board: "I am not hostile," he was saying to the Duce and his hierarchs, "why are you attacking me?"

She has donned a pair of glasses, Sara De Viesti, and with them on she leafs through her notes, and continues:

"Even in the ending of his first detective novel, in 1935, he throws in something patriotic and Fascist: one of the protagonists, burned by the tragic story that Commissioner De Vincenzi has solved with the usual deftness of a gracious and literate detective, opts for an adventure and volunteers to fight in Ethiopia, to make Italy into an empire... a nice redemption, no?"

But then there was everything that irritated the regime. The rules were clear. In Italian detective stories, the murderer had better not be Italian. Suicides became mysterious deaths, or car accidents, no one takes their own life in the lictorian paradise! And the scoundrel or the murderer was never, never, never meant to get away with it. The honor of the Fascist police would have gone down the drain, letting a culprit escape under their noses!

De Angelis had had to adapt, but you could see him forcing it; his books were full of Misses O'Brian, Messrs. Bolton, adventurers who had committed crimes in South Africa, people named Shanahan, or Crestansen . . . a heavy lift, having them live in Milan . . .

They went on for hours. Every word was a detail that was added to the picture, every single episode, every quote, became for Manlio Parrini a new brushstroke to give to his light, to the film that was taking shape. Maybe it was taking too much shape.

At dinnertime, he opened his arms disconsolately, there was nothing there in the house for two people to eat, only to drink. And he didn't want to go out, with the risk of running into some other nosy person in search of the Maestro's opinion on the murder of the widow Bastoni. So Sara De Viesti took the matter in hand and she also took her phone in hand, and within less than half an hour they had in front of them, still on the table in front of the sofa, a perfect Indian dinner, with the scents of curry and cumin jumping out of the greasy wrappers.

Waiting for the order to arrive, Sara De Viesti had scrolled through the online newspapers, just to take a break, get away from the thirties, and return to the real world.

"Your crime is holding court," she said, laughing. Then she read him the page from the *Corriere*, the digital edition. The title was "No Seizure in the Villa of Mysteries" and it said, in a few lines, that the investigators had searched the villa, yes, sealed it shut, of course, but they had not removed anything, neither documents nor evidence, and the thing seemed strange, strange enough to turn it into the headline. Manlio Parrini had smiled, but had not explained anything, neither his meeting with the reporter nor the request that Sensini had made of him. Explaining would have taken time, and he wanted to go back there, to the thirties, didn't want to lose the thread of that fabric they were weaving in tandem, as duelers, as a couple.

Not now, anyway, when they had reached the point they both knew they had to get to. The murder, the end of Augusto De Angelis, the beating on the lakefront in Bellagio, on July 2, 1944.

Here Sara De Viesti turned wary, because she claimed that the case was closed, and took one of her folders in her hand, the one with DEATH written on it, and inside a few crumpled sheets, underlined in pencil, or shaded by a fluorescent highlighter.

"I told you. It's not a cold case, the case is solved."

"Someone is alive, and then he's dead, Sara, the case is never solved."

"By law," she says.

Manlio Parrini looked up at the ceiling, held his breath for a while, and then made his speech.

"I couldn't give a fuck about the law, Sara. Or about the courts. I read the biographies; I read some reconstructions. That story is not at all clear. That someone wanted to put a stop to it, I get that. Truncate it and nod off. Forget, move on to something else, life goes on. But there was a murder, and it is a murder that went unpunished. And everything we have said all day about the victim of this murder, the climate, the light, the compromises, the concessions, the truths, the lies, the press releases, the detective stories, the Milan of the bourgeois interiors, the gloomy Milan of the night exterior... Everything, everything, tells us that story must be told. Everything, damn it! It has to be dug up. Invented, if you will. But it all has to come out in its totally banal glory." He had almost screamed.

That was understandable, he was defending his film, his idea. He was defending the "light" he had decided to give it.

"We'll talk more about it tomorrow," she said.

It was very late, almost one o'clock, she was tired, and he was too, they had been talking and working for almost twelve hours. And that aspect of the thing, the murder of Augusto De Angelis, had to be treated with lucidity, without eyes that were drooping, without any concessions to fatigue, without avoiding discussion.

They arranged to meet the following day, after lunch as usual, and she piled up her things, books, folders, documents, in a small, almost orderly pyramid. She practically rushed out of the house, the time to wait for a taxi, because she didn't want to waste time on goodbyes and farewells. The annex of the Bastoni villa seemed empty to him, without that bushy head of red hair, without that voice interrupting him, contradicting him.

Manlio Parrini had gone to sleep.

The bed is behind a movable wall, a bookcase filled on both sides, that hides, although not completely, the sleeping area from the rest. But he didn't sleep well. He tossed and turned, he thought, he woke up. He was thinking of the "light," of that happy and frightened feeling when your blank canvas fills up and with every brushstroke the doubts and questions increase. Would he succeed? Would he bring that film home the way he wanted it? Not a film about a detective story writer from the thirties, but a film about us, about dark times, about the dictatorship of conformism, about our small concessions of spaces of freedom because they seem to us to be negligible details. This was the precious passage, this was the touch of Monsieur Parrinì.

The Indian dinner has its side effects, though. An unquenchable thirst, a need for liquids. So, he looks at the alarm clock, it's ten minutes to four. He gets up, not without a certain seventy-year-old effort, and reaches the refrigerator. He doesn't turn on the light, it's not pitch dark and the curtains on the large window let in a bit of light from outside, moonlight. In his underwear, in front of the open refrigerator, drinking greedily from a plastic bottle, Manlio Parrini hears a thud. Like something hitting the ground. Then an imperceptible crunching of the gravel in the driveway, in the garden. Maybe he imagined the crunching, but not the thud, he heard that well. He looked at his watch, 3:57. Then he almost ran to the curtain, five quick steps, and he pushed it away slowly.

A black silhouette moved from the wall next to the gate and walked slowly to one side of the villa, then disappeared. Whoever it is, he has climbed over the wall, thought Parrini, who is now awake and alert, whipped to attention by adrenaline and surprise.

So, he grabbed a chair and placed himself behind the curtain, artfully opened a few more inches, but he didn't see or hear anything more. No light came on, no silhouette moved. Nothing at all. He was left alone, him, the chair, and the watch, which he checked at short intervals for two hours.

Six o'clock. It's early, he said to himself.

Half past six. It is still early.

At ten minutes to seven he couldn't resist and looked for a number in the memory of his cell phone. A voice answered immediately, after just one ring. Not a question, just a quick and very clear syllable:

"Yes."

"Prosecutor Sensini? Parrini, do you remem—"

"Parrini, of course, good morning, Maestro, do you think this is a time to disturb a lady?"

It's clear that she was awake, operational, already ironic despite the dawn.

"A lady, I don't know, but a deputy prosecutor..." Then he told her about the nocturnal intrusion, about the silhouette that was moving warily in the courtyard, about the fact that he had mounted guard but nothing more had happened.

"Don't move from home, I'll be there later this morning," she said.

Then the phone went dead, Manlio Parrini abandoned his chair and his window on the courtyard and went back to bed. Now, yes, he slept.

He even dreamed. Sara De Viesti dressed as Josephine Baker leaving for Ethiopia.

Crazy old man.

11

TWO CARS FULL OF MEN, SOME IN UNIFORM, OTHERS IN plain clothes. They entered the villa, led by Deputy Prosecutor Sensini and the deputy police chief, the one he had seen before.

Manlio Parrini looks into the courtyard pushing the curtain aside, it's half past eight, it seems that they are trotting inside like sheep running into the paddock, pushed by the shepherd dog. He expected the sound of the doorbell, with Sensini at the door, instead they went right to the villa, and no one had come by his place.

He would like to get to work, read the papers that are sticking out of Sara De Viesti's bag, or start tearing down the small pyramid of books, documents, and folders that she left there. But he can't concentrate. He waits. He moves the chair next to the window again and makes himself comfortable, so that he has a view of the garden, he flips through the newspapers on the iPad. That gadget has also relieved him of the inconvenience of walking a few hundred yards, up to the newsstand. Who knows, maybe if he had a dog, he would start getting his hands dirty with ink again.

To his great surprise, the investigation into the murder of the widow Bastoni has a lot of space, because there is news. "Bastoni Murder: Suspect Held" headlines *La Repubblica*. And *La Stampa* even puts the story on the front page: "Turning Point in the Bastoni Murder: An Arrest During the Night."

So, he read on avidly, but there wasn't much more to it than what the headline said. The arrestee is G.F., auto electrician, forty-two years old, wife and two children, resident in Milan, no known record. He will be questioned today, the prosecutor's office did not provide details.

In the local news pages there is a photo of him, of him the Maestro, of Manlio Parrini. Small, not recent, from when he was twenty and maybe even thirty years younger, and he laughs to see himself so young, on the set. Some reporter writes that next to the villa of the murder—it is written just like that, "the villa of the murder"—lives the famous director of *Broken Truths*, Manlio Parrini, who, however, did not want to make a statement. The other romanticizes a bit about it, says that perhaps he, the famous director, saw something, which is a rather stupid stretch, that he has certainly been questioned, and that when invited to speak to reporters a woman who was with him had rebuffed them rather brusquely. Sara De Viesti's red hair roamed the room for a few moments while Parrini remembered the scene of the day before, with a small shake of the head and boundless admiration for the woman.

Well, the damage seems limited, because the novelty of the detainee, the fact that there is a suspect, even an arrest, is the highlight of the day.

Then he moved on to the *Corriere* with some apprehension. A full page, in the local news section, on the murder of widow Bastoni. Manlio Parrini scrolls through it quickly, there is not much more than what he had read online yesterday with Sara, while they were poisoning themselves with the Indian dinner. Obviously, the headline is on the arrest of the night before, even if here there is no tone of a solved case and caution prevails. Claudio Tarsi, the reporter who had followed him to the trattoria, who had offered him lunch, had kept his word. In every sense. He quoted him, yes, he could not fail to do so since the other newspapers had the news, but without photographs from his golden era and without emphasis: his presence in the courtyard of the crime was declassified to a small curiosity, an added attraction, nothing more. Rightly, indeed, the fact that he lived there, close to Villa Bastoni, was noted in relation to the fact that his old patron, the victim's husband, had in the past financed one of his films, the most beautiful, the most acclaimed, and certainly it was in that way that a friendship was born...

Oh well, a little embroidery did no harm.

Their pact had been respected, in short, but even more: his leak about the investigations, about the search of the villa, about the fact that the investigators had not removed anything, the lie that Sensini had suggested to him, had even become the title of a short column: "Investigations in the Dark." It deplored the failure of the prosecutor's office to keep the press informed, complained that Sensini, although competent and experienced, as evidenced by other investigations successfully closed, had not even called a press conference, although it is hoped that today, with a suspect detained, we may get to know a little more.

Then in one line—an obvious message to the prosecutor's office—it was emphasized that the doubts of the press about the management of the case were legitimate, because it appeared that the investigators had not removed probative elements from the villa, papers or documents, which must have been there, and that they had limited themselves to seizing and sealing everything, leaving behind potentially interesting material.

"Unusual, to say the least," concluded the piece, only initialed, C.T.

• • •

Outside, in the courtyard, everything is quiet.

At a quarter past ten, finally, Sensini and her deputy police chief crossed the garden, made the white pebbles crunch, and rang his doorbell.

After an icy handshake, the deputy chief remained standing next to the entrance while Sensini sat on the sofa, in her usual place, and looked at him with eyes asking for clarifications and a cup of coffee. Then she dismissed the policeman, who returned to the villa. Manlio Parrini pushed the curtain aside for a second, and saw Carlos in the garden, waiting, with a lady, a certain Enrica, the cook-housekeeper, perhaps about to collect her things from the scene of the crime, or perhaps summoned for a new, more stringent interrogation.

"Thank you," said the deputy prosecutor. "You gave us a big hand."

She's referring to the fake news published by the *Corriere*, about the failure of the investigators to seize the material useful for the investigation, left in the villa.

Now Manlio Parrini is a bit amazed. He'd expected a barrage. Who had he seen climbing over the courtyard wall that night? At what time? What had the intruder done? How did he leave? But nothing. He thought he had helped the investigation, with his Hitchcockian stakeout, but instead she didn't ask him anything.

He resists for a few minutes, brings coffee, sits down, and...

"Well? Aren't you going to tell me anything?"

Sensini made a little laugh and explained.

"Yes, you gave us a hand, Parrini, you helped us set a small trap. We put some cameras in there," she indicates the villa with a vague gesture toward the garden, "and now, the intruder who woke you up last night, we are going to pick him up, he'll have several things to explain, why enter a building under judicial seizure, which is, moreover, the scene of a crime, at night, climbing over a wall, it's not exactly something normal..."

"And who is it?"

Silence.

Manlio Parrini is looking on at a fight that is all happening inside himself. He has not yet figured out if his being an instrument of a trap set by the investigators is an ethically justifiable move, let's say that for the moment he has put the question on hold. But in short, it helped them, didn't it? And he also proved himself to be reliable, he didn't reveal anything to the guy from the *Corriere* about his meeting with Sensini, mute as a fish, apart from the detail that she suggested that he reveal... And now he gets in return... nothing?

He is a little annoyed, and he doesn't hide it. On the contrary, he decides to go on the attack.

"You don't say anything to me... You don't tell me, even if I'm playing on your side... That's pretty unfair, eh!"

"Parrini, you know how these things go, the investigation is confidential..."

"Right, speaking of confidentiality... Why don't you tell me about the two strands of a woman's hair found on the victim? Or the murderer who drank coffee with the widow Bastoni before strangling her?"

It's a low blow. Sensini takes the hit, but it is clear that she is not happy. "Shit," she says, and becomes thoughtful. "How do you know these things?"

Some of her people have talked, she thinks, but it's obvious, there was a crowd in there, if you count the people from Forensics, the uniformed officers, the coroner...

"That Tarsi, the reporter who helped you by publishing the press release that you suggested to me... He's the one. He says that the case is complicated even for reasons... Let's say political reasons, even if perhaps that's not the right word, that not everything can be published, but the blond hairs on the victim, and even the cups on the desk at the scene of the crime, are rather precise details, not things someone made up."

Now Deputy Prosecutor Chiara Sensini has a worried face that says a lot of things. This we didn't need, it says, and also: oh shit, you can see she is assessing the damage of that leaked information, the consequences it could have for her investigation. All condensed into a single facial expression.

He figured he had won the point.

"So? Who was the intruder who woke me up last night?"

She put her coffee cup down on the table, amid Sara De Viesti's papers, and looked at him for a long moment. Soon everything will be public, perhaps it is not a great risk to keep someone who helped them informed... And then she decides.

"Matteo D'Onofrio, the nephew of the murdered old lady... of the victim, grandnephew, or rather, in short, the son of the famous banker, or whatever he is. He forced open a shutter at the back of the villa, this morning at five past four, went looking for something in the study, there is a filing cabinet and a closet full of papers... that is, there was, before we took the papers away, of course."

"What an idiot."

"Well, yes, definitely. You see, trusting the press? He must have read the *Corriere* yesterday, the online edition, and decided it was a good time to look for something in his great-aunt's archive. What, we don't know yet, but we'll know soon, because there's an arrest warrant out for him that will be executed in minutes..."

The grandnephew, thinks Manlio Parrini. And the foreign handyman. And the gloomy villa that seems to attract everyone like honey does flies.

"It's looking more and more like a De Angelis plot, you know? Well, apart from the cameras, of course, but..."

Then another thing comes to mind, which is out of tune, doesn't fit in.

"And the arrested suspect?" he asks.

In the whole affair, which smells of family feud a mile away, the auto electrician does not fit in in any way.

Sensini answers with a question.

"What do you know about the affairs of the widow Bastoni, Maestro?"

"Well, I would say nothing, what I read in the newspapers. Real estate, I think, a lot of apartments, offices, all income-generating, a good fortune, it would seem."

"That's right, but with some variants that are not exactly legal..."

"Can you tell me, or should I call my friend at the *Corriere* and get him to tell me what he cannot write?"

Sensini got up, pushed the curtain aside, and looked out. In the courtyard there was still Carlos, the Indigenous cube, sitting on the wall of the waterless fountain, the maid Enrica was no longer to be seen, the policemen were all inside the villa, perhaps the woman was collecting her luggage and answering the questions of the deputy chief. She sat down again and began to speak, as if to make a summary, perhaps she too needed to repeat herself.

"About seventy apartments, offices and other buildings, shops, laboratories, things like that, investments of the deceased husband. Income-generating with a perfect system... How much would you pay in rent for a three-room apartment in Porta Romana, Parrini? Fifteen hundred? Two thousand? Well, all the contracts are regular, all the payments into three current accounts of the victim are very punctual, traceable, transparent, but... Three hundred euros in rent? Four hundred and fifty for a workshop? Twenty-five thousand euros a year for just over seventeen thousand square feet of offices in Corso Sempione? Is there anything that doesn't add up for you, Maestro?"

"I don't know anything about rents, but it doesn't seem like much to me... very little for a city like Milan, let's say that we are at a quarter, a fifth, of market prices."

"Exactly. Everything else under the table, in cash, in person, which explains, among other things, the comings and goings at the villa and the fact that old lady Bastoni had a kind of office, on the ground floor, the place where they strangled her."

"Well, that's a hypothesis."

"No, Parrini, it's not a hypothesis, because in the closets and filing cabinets... the same ones where the young grandnephew went rummaging last night, we found the accounting... Let's say the real one, not the official one that her accountant gave us. All perfect, that one, including tax returns, leases, and bank transfers... the over the table part, let's say... The under the table part was kept at the villa. So tidy and perfect that it took us just a couple of days to verify it. Each tenant with a regular contract corresponds to a folder with the real accounts... One paid, say, eight thousand a year and then paid the widow Bastoni fifteen or twenty thousand under the table, sometimes in installments of three months, others yearly..."

"What madness, and no one has ever said anything? No complaints?"

"Oh, there must have been some protests, now we are hearing them one by one... but nothing that reached us, at the prosecutor's office, I mean. Maybe the old woman was skilled with evictions, and then people think twice before making trouble... you know, Parrini, not everyone has an annex like yours, finding a house in Milan is not a walk in the park."

"It seemed like a De Angelis detective story, but here we are raising the bar," says Manlio Parrini now. "We are at Raskolnikov and Dostoevsky's old usurer!"

"Lucky you, that you can laugh."

"And the detainee, then? Let me guess! A student from St. Petersburg turned auto electrician!"

"Will you stop?" she said. But she laughed a little. "The auto electrician, Giovanni Furlan, is one of those who didn't go along. He was behind on his payments, and one fine morning he came to quarrel with the old woman about his debts and unpaid rent, the under the table, because the official ones are very punctual."

"Is that enough to arrest him?"

"Well, you know, Maestro, it was the morning of the murder, eleven o'clock, more or less, and the autopsy certifies that the woman died between nine and noon. He says the door was open, he went in and saw the lady lying on the ground. He was scared, he says, but not enough, perhaps, because instead of alerting the police or calling for help, he started rummaging through the closet, found the folder with his name on it, took it, and left."

"And you believe it?"

"We don't believe anything, Parrini. We believe evidence and look for it. Of course, it's not a very good situation, his, but I questioned him all night, I had just finished when you called me this morning and..."

"Don't tell me! Intuition!"

She looked at him steadily for a moment, caught up in some thoughts.

"Aren't you exaggerating a bit with the familiarity?" she asked him, point-blank. More than a reproach.

"You're right, excuse me. And how did you find out, if no one saw him come and go?"

"There were seventy-two tenants in the official accounting of the old lady, the one in the hands of the accountant, the clean one. And only seventy-one folders in the real accounting, the one locked in the closet of the villa. It wasn't hard, let's say, and once we understood who was missing, we felt a great desire to ask him a question or two... But first we took a look at his telephone records and... in short... His cell phone connected with this zone, here where we are, between ten to eleven and twenty past eleven on the day of the crime. So, the questions to ask him became four, and even more."

"What an idiot. Another one! It's an epidemic!"

"Yes, what an idiot. Moreover, he left a footprint in the closet he rummaged in. Say what you want, Parrini, but someone who goes to kill the old usurer, if we want to stick with your Raskolnikov reference, does not carry a telephone and generally does not leave footprints around."

"Maybe he didn't know he was going to kill her? . . . A brazen fit of rage?"

This time she let out a really hearty laugh. Finally.

"Let's drop it, Maestro. I've told you too much. Our pact of silence remains, however. Now give me a glass of water and I'll go."

"And the coffee with the murderer? The other mysterious clue? The strands of a woman's hair?"

"Don't press your luck too far, Maestro, be satisfied for today."

"And you stop calling me Maestro."

Then Deputy Prosecutor Sensini received a phone call, a very short one, it must have been a work call. She nodded and said, "Good," nothing else. Then she made a call, with Manlio Parrini pretending not to listen, in which she gave cut-and-dried instructions:

"Keep him there. Really? His problem. Of course, the lawyer, yes. Let them wait, there's not much more here, anyway, it'll be another hour or two."

"The grandnephew?"

"Yes, it's up to me to question him. He has a sprained ankle. If even twenty-five-year-olds don't know how to climb over a wall anymore, we're in bad shape, Maestro."

It was time for goodbyes and ceremonies, and therefore the time when there would be neither, because neither he nor she are ceremonial types. But when she had almost reached the door, Sensini's phone rang again, and when she looked at the display, she made a face like the one you make when you can't find your house keys in your pocket, a mixture of annoyance and discouragement.

"Excuse me," she whispered to Parrini, and then answered.

"Shoot, boss."

Then silence, just her listening. And then her answering. "You see, boss, he climbed over a wall to enter a building subject to seizure where there was a murder . . ."

Silence again.

"But what press! Have you ever seen me talk to the press about an ongoing investigation?"

She raised her voice a little, not too much, but pretty much when you're talking to the chief prosecutor of the Republic of Milan.

Silence again.

"But what the fuck do I care about the famous politico and his lawyers . . . even if it's the entire bar of the Court of Milan . . . Someone sneaks into a murder scene and I have to pretend nothing happened? You're joking, aren't you, boss? The minister's phone call? What do you think I should do?"

Still silence, but the other guy must have softened his tone a bit, he spoke for a good minute while Sensini turned red in the face, furious.

"Of course, boss, all the prudence necessary. Sure. I understand."

Somehow they had signed a truce, anyone would have understood that, even hearing only one side of the phone call as he had.

"The top brass is calling in the artillery, eh!" said Parrini.

"Shut up, please, this is not the time."

"Eh," he said with a smile, "broken truths."

She already had one hand on the door handle, but she turned around and looked straight at him, a look that she perhaps reserved for the most hardheaded defendants.

"Manlio, fuck off."

12

SARA DE VIESTI CALLED, SHE'LL BE THERE LATER, SHE has an idea for the first scene of the film, she wants to propose it to him, but she is following a lead, she says that it'll work only if she finds certain documents. So now Manlio Parrini is studying, he has lined up the material to read, and he has a list to check off. He starts with that.

First of all, the places.

De Angelis's Milan, that is, the Milan of Inspector De Vincenzi, is already in itself a character in the film. It is a small, tiny Milan, little more than the ring of the Navigli canals, and since his stories are almost always bourgeois stories, of high society and fat cats, and bankers, and well-heeled doctors with lots of lovers, and diaphanous and filiform young women, it is all within a stone's throw. From Piazza San Fedele, where the police headquarters used to be, to the cathedral, to the streets of Brera, to Corso Littorio, which today is called Corso Matteotti, because it's not only history that corrects its mistakes, but toponymy also has its say.

For his investigations, De Vincenzi often moves around on foot or takes the streetcar for a few stops, or rather the trolley, or a taxi, or rather, a *tassì*, as it had to be said at the time.

But that area that today is the city's showcase with all the same shops that could be in Oslo or Paris, Berlin or Madrid, with the bright screens of winking advertisements hanging on the cathedral, was at the time a maze of dark streets, shadows, figures fading into the fog. Yes, De Vincenzi's Milan is dark, it is obscure, it is a small Gotham City, in spite of its international allure and the directives of the regime, according to which crime did not exist and was not to be talked about.

That's the first step, Parrini thinks, the gloomy and murky air must then explode into the lights of the interiors, except in the inspector's den, in that damp, flaking-plaster room with the black telephone and the desk piled with papers, under which, when someone appears at the door, he hides his beloved books.

So, the director of photography must be a master of shadows, of chiaroscuro, one who has a steady hand in the changes of light, of tone. His old pal Sastri? He must be eighty years old. Will he feel like embarking on an adventure like this? Or that young guy whose work he has seen lately, amazed that, at that age, not even thirty years old, he already had his own fluid resolve, his own nuanced approach, because darkness is a color...he doesn't remember the name, he takes a note, a scribble: "Ask Sara."

Then the bell rang—that place is becoming a seaport—and it was a somewhat disoriented courier, because outside the gate there was a car full of cops who asked him where he was going, what he wanted; a third degree just to deliver a package.

Manlio Parrini opens the big yellow envelope. It comes from the production company, Luca Corrioni's StratoFilm. Faces, he thinks.

Corrioni has read Sara De Viesti's synopsis, the long, detailed one, and it gave him a first impression. It's not time for faces yet, Parrini says to himself, but since he has it in hand, the envelope with the photographs, he might as well take a look. There are several folders, one for each proposed role. He looks at the women, only because it is the folder that happened into his hands first. Beautiful women, beautiful girls. He strives to see them made up as he would like them to be, the bobbed hair, the clothes of the time, in short, he strives to translate them.

He looks for the face of the woman that interests him most, the one of the betrayal, in the final scene. Hers has to be a different face, the face of an ordinary woman, not of the Milanese jet set who sashay between

La Scala and the Gallery. We will have to work on it, he thinks, she is an actress who will have only one scene, maybe two, but she's fundamental, she's . . . then he sees her, she looks perfect. Irma Grotti. Irma, even her name is from the thirties, he thinks. He reads her résumé. The girl is no longer a girl, she has played several interesting roles, a series on some platform, a bit of theater. He puts the photo aside for when they do the auditions.

Then he moves on to the men. Some of them he knows, actors he has seen in films, in some commercials. Ugo Semballi, about whom he's heard a lot of good things, a big man with a good-natured look about him who could be a perfect Cruni, the faithful cop to whom De Vincenzi entrusts the most delicate operations, a kind of right-hand man. He too will have his audition, but Parrini has a good feeling, and believes that in this case it'll be a sure thing.

There's only one envelope left, the most important one, the one of the possible leading man. Of course, Parrini already has names in mind. Saverio Protti, first of all, who jumps between theater and artsy cinema. A cultured actor who does not sink to the rubbish that is fashionable now. And he also likes Tullio Vinerga, because he has his own fluid way of moving on camera, an expressive face, so much so that sometimes you don't need lines, just the face. He had asked Corrioni to check that they were not already under contract, that they did not have any series in the works or, worse, an entire theatrical season already underway...

But the last envelope is not heavy at all. It's even too light. It contains a printed letter and three set photographs, all of the same person. The face doesn't mean anything to him... Yes, a face he's seen, of course, but he wouldn't be able to say in which film. The pronounced jaw, the blue eyes, a handsome man with an alluring look.

This is not his Augusto De Angelis, that's for sure.

He has no torment, doesn't have the eyes that a bourgeois Italian of the thirties should have, the eyes of someone crushed by an obtuse and ignorant regime. Steven Highner is the name. A long list of titles follows, films that Parrini has not seen.

He reads the letter.

Dear Parrini,
As you can see, I got to work with my team. Don't worry: everyone is sworn to the utmost confidentiality. The bad news is that we still don't have a script, even if the synopsis that De Viesti gave me is pretty detailed and renders the idea of what we want to do...

We want? Parrini said to himself while reading. He feels a bit of irritation rising, but he still can't put his finger on it, there is not enough meat on the fire to say that the meat stinks and is making him sick.

Speaking of De Viesti, you know that I respect her a lot, but her, let's say, underground reputation doesn't provide enough assurances to producers and institutional financiers. I would suggest that she be flanked by a more popular screenwriter, someone like Gaslini, or Stranni, who has had some great ratings for series broadcast on national networks...

He wasn't mistaken. The meat really does stink.

In practice, Corrioni is talking about sidelining his screenwriter, softening everything, rounding all the edges like they do for a TV series.

He put the letter on the table, amid his and Sara De Viesti's sweaty papers, grabbed the iPad, and typed something. His disappointment has turned to anger. Aldo Gaslini has written two potboilers, bad copies of French comedies. And Stranni, talk about trying to draw blood from a turnip. She has made a name for herself with those biopics that are all the rage today, the great scientist, the great explorer, all monotonous and flat as the tundra, hagiographic, reassuring.

His blood is simmering, but Parrini knows that it is not over yet. The bitter pill is right there in front of him, in the form of a printed sheet. He picks it up again.

After swearing her to absolute secrecy, I also talked about the project to Sanna Berry, the famous producer, you know her, right? Don't take things too lightly,

Maestro, convincing Americans to coproduce an Italian costume drama is no cinch. However, they would be interested in the return behind the camera of the great Manlio Parrini, and advise (more than advise) taking Highner as the lead. Attached are his photos and film credits. They already have him under contract, he is on the launching pad now and there is a lot of talk about him. For the American market he would have a big impact, which is important, and in my opinion he could be a perfect De Angelis.

Now I'll let you think about it, Maestro, naturally you know where to find me here for any questions you have about our film.

Warm regards,
Luca Corrioni

To get really angry, to be irate, to live in the fury of rage, you really have to be young. Instead, Manlio Parrini, who is not young at all, is just a pissed-off old man, a gentleman who is over seventy and who is now almost screaming, alone, cursing and swearing while hissing filth and profanity.

Asshole. Assholes. They don't understand shit.

They were taking his story, the story of yesterday, which is the story of today, which is the story of always, and making it into box-office entertainment, a Hollywood blockbuster, the usual bullshit. With an angry gesture, he grabbed the iPad and typed "Steven Highner video." It turned up some trailers and film clips. He was a guy who chased, on foot, airplanes in takeoff, who played a sniper hitting tiny black silhouettes miles away, who was the corrupt lawyer in a mafia movie. Then various scattered headlines: "Highner, New Sex Symbol" or "Hollywood Has a New Idol."

It was garbage. It was shit. It was nothing but market.

Now Manlio Parrini picks up his phone and sends a message to Sara De Viesti:

"Where the fuck are you?"

Not even a minute passes and the answer arrives: "Good mood, eh! :))) The thing took longer than I thought, see you tomorrow. But check your mail, I sent you a message. Then I'll tell you about my idea for the opening scene. See you tomorrow."

He wanted to share his anger with her, his discouragement, to vent, to see her stiffen, to talk about it with her. Flank her with someone who would normalize her...he was anticipating her "fuck yous!" and her "shitheads!"

And instead nothing, he would have to wait until tomorrow.

He picks up the iPad and opens his mail. The message from Sara De Viesti has an attachment, but first he reads what she's written as the subject: "Look what I found!"

He opens the pdf, it is a yellowed sheet, half typewritten and half written by hand.

Milano, 4 / II / 41 / XIX

AUGUSTO DE ANGELIS
"The mystery of Cinecittà"

Report:
This novel by De Angelis shows his usual skill in treating the detective novel.

The characters are spontaneous and full of life, the environment and atmosphere are rendered effectively, and the detective story, properly so-called, is quite new. There are some defects, such as, for example, the excessive number of people whose actions are influenced by some form, more or less serious, of mental imbalance, but on the whole the novel seems to me passable.

In the event that the book is proposed for the five-lire detective stories, the judgment of Dr. Piceni is naturally necessary.

This was the typewritten part. Below, in pen, Dr. Piceni's note:

It is not a great job, but it is acceptable: it would only be necessary for De Angelis to make some adjustments—

not serious—in certain somewhat murky points. It is more a matter of verbal expressions than anything else, and I think there will be no difficulties.
*E. E. Piceni**

Manlio Parrini reads the yellowed sheet. He reads it twice, three times. Enrico Piceni is an important name in the history of Italian publishing. A great translator, a talent scout, respected by all. For years, for decades, he engaged in a wise, intelligent hand-to-hand fight with the censorship of the regime, which opposed foreign translations, which demanded that the texts be adapted, which controlled everything. The practice was that the author adapted to the times, that he was careful, in short, not to disturb the regime's sleep too much. Then the readers' reports took care of it, a task of the publisher, who advised, refined, pointed out the things that could hinder publication. "Some adjustments," the "somewhat murky points."

Then the manuscript passed to the control of the Ministry, which could give the green light for publication or block it.

* The reading opinion is contained in Fondazione Arnoldo e Alberto Mondadori Milano, Archivio storico Arnoldo Mondadori editore, Segreteria editoriale estero, Giudizi favorevoli anni Trenta, folder 1, file 62 (Augusto De Angelis).

Three censorings, thinks Manlio Parrini. Broken freedoms, all right. Broken three times.

But holding on to that document, which Sara had gone to find in the most precious and remote archives, right at that moment, just after reading the producer's letter, had a strong significance, a kind of revelation. Didn't the censorings and self-censorings of the early forties resemble in a crystalline, almost grotesque, way those of today? Then, there was Pavolini, an obtuse bureaucrat of what can be said and not said, now there's the production machine: someone to work alongside Sara De Viesti to make her digestible, the trendy actor to attract money... Wasn't it the same thing in the end? A check, a putting the author in his place, a... Parrini reread the sheet... a "some adjustments."

The anger of before has turned into a cold, murderous determination. This is one more reason to make it, the film, because it increasingly seems to him a film about today, about what can and cannot be said. Oh, of course, without party officials saluting and clicking their heels, without jail, and without people beating you to death, but...

He was not hungry, but he had to eat something. So he put on a jacket, checked that he had the keys, his wallet, his cigarettes, and went out, he was surprised to find a gentle breeze, which perhaps was announcing rain, but which at the moment caressed him gently.

He started walking slowly toward the city center, mulling over the things that were piling up, one on top of the other. The film was taking shape, and indeed every day he was finding new reasons for making it, and the anger he had felt earlier was becoming one more reason.

The light is dimming, the days are getting shorter, the cold is on its way along with frequent rain, which will be here soon. The fog, no, that's a thing of the past, it has gone out of fashion too, what a shame. It was still there in the detective stories of Augusto De Angelis, or in the ones by Giorgio Scerbanenco; it gave them a mysterious and lugubrious touch, when the figures turned into shadows. Now there is only a blue twilight broken by the sounds and lights of traffic, the shops closed with the windows still illuminated, the bars full of people sipping late aperitifs, by now aperi-dinners, celebrating the end of the working day.

Shadows aren't part of the current scene, they're old hat, like him.

13

"OUR CLIENT WILL CLARIFY EVERYTHING, AND WE ARE sure that this misunderstanding will be resolved very shortly." Matteo D'Onofrio, or rather his father, Vincenzo D'Onofrio, the grand marshal, the powerful nephew of the old Bastoni, the one for whom the chief prosecutor had intervened so heavily and the minister had made a phone call, has fielded a team of big-time lawyers. Their statements in the newspapers are of confident expectation: everything will deflate, the investigating magistrate will not confirm the arrest, the boy remains available for questioning and to provide information requested by the prosecutor's office, total faith in the system of justice, etc., etc. As usual Claudio Tarsi managed to have something more, putting the *Corriere* one step ahead of the competition. Manlio Parrini is surprised to feel a certain admiration for that rough-hewn hulk of a man, who evidently knows his business when it comes to breaking people's balls. In short, not that he reveals to his readers some spectacular scoop, just a few more nuances, but in some cases nuances are everything. Why had the young man entered the sealed villa after a crime? An error in judgment, a prank, he was overwhelmed by the violent death of his beloved great-aunt. Okay, but what was his motive...? Who knows what's going on in the mind of a shaken and grieving boy... Anyway, he did not steal anything, he just wanted to see the place where the old woman had been killed. What kind of relationship did the young D'Onofrio have with the victim? Excellent, he was the old lady's only nephew, that is, grandnephew, he went to visit her often, he had even been to the villa the evening before the murder...

In short, the line is that he is a poor, confused boy, nothing to do with the murder.

Maliciously, in a short column next to the interview with the lawyers, initialed C.T., the newspaper wonders why the old woman's grandnephew, who had been at the villa the day before the crime, had not been questioned, and if by chance the prosecutor's office has reserved special treatment for a family like the D'Onofrios. Incidentally, the auto electrician Giovanni Furlan, who had stolen material from the scene of the crime with the body still warm on the floor, remains in prison while the young D'Onofrio was immediately placed under house arrest. He lives at his mother's house, in a beautiful penthouse in Via Vittorio Veneto, with windows overlooking the park.

The law is equal for everyone, Parrini thinks, but for auto electricians it is a little less equal than for the children of VIPs.

Another newspaper has a short interview with the boy's girlfriend, a Swiss fashion model. She is sure that everything will be cleared up, they're planning to get married in February, then they will live in Basel, where she has a small cosmetics brand and he has a position already reserved for him on the upper floors of one of the Confederation's banks. It is getting to be more and more a novel by De Angelis, thinks Manlio Parrini, the banker and the beautiful foreigner are perfect additions to the cast of characters.

In other words, Sensini had not succeeded in keeping the matter of the deceased's grandnephew under the radar, or perhaps she had not wanted to. Parrini could see that you can hide some clues, but not the detention of a suspect, especially in the presence of overwhelming evidence such as a video that shows him breaking the seals and entering the scene of a crime at four in the morning.

There has to be some tension circulating in the prosecutor's office, all the newspapers were asking for a press conference, deploring the silence in such a striking case. Sensini, in a brief note that they all published, had explained that the investigation was continuing, that there was a lot of evidence to be checked and verified and that in due time...

A predictable ballet.

Manlio Parrini had started the day like this, with coffee, leafing through the newspapers, and his first cigarette, but then, and it was just a quarter past eight, the intercom, the one at the gate, rang and a police officer, young and very polite, showed up at his door with a sheet of paper in his hand. It was a kind of invitation—or perhaps a summons, what a highfalutin word—to present himself at the prosecutor's office, and he, the boy in uniform, was there to accompany him. The other was in the car.

Manlio Parrini doesn't know what to think: he is a bit amused by his being in a car with two cops driving across town, even if they have neither a siren nor a flashing light. It is still a white and blue car, the service radio is crackling, and the driving is definitely sporty, to say the least.

Riding along nearly the whole time in silence, they reached the Palace of Justice, then the young policeman accompanied him through corridors and elevators, on those marble floors, among that buzz of people waiting for hearings and judgments, mostly lawyers and clerks, walking up and down them. At ten past nine he was sitting in a small but pleasant room, with the photo of the president of the Republic hanging on one wall, a guy sitting behind a computer, and Deputy Prosecutor Chiara Sensini at her desk, looking at him with a strange smile. They shook hands and nothing else while the other guy rattled off his personal details, reading them off a sheet of paper . . . Manlio Parrini, born in . . . on the . . . resident in . . . Was that him? Is that right? Yes. Here as a person informed of the facts . . .

Then she spoke.

"Excuse me for the inconvenience, Maestro, but it's time to do things by the book, and then there is some news about you that has emerged from the investigation . . ."

You should see Parrini's face now.

Some news about him? Which is to say? Sensini notices his astonishment and almost laughs, perhaps it must seem absurd even to her that he is there on that chair although they had chatted almost as friends on his sofa, in the living room of the annex full of papers and books, with him offering her coffee.

The morning of the murder, September 6, he had woken up as usual, had breakfast, and read the newspapers, then worked a little on his film project. Afterward, he had gone out . . .

"What time?"

"I don't know exactly, half past eleven, noon? I called a taxi, the exact time should be recorded somewhere."

"Do you know that the murder has been traced back to an unspecified hour between nine and noon?"

"Yes, I read the newspapers..." He was about to say, "Yes, you told me," but he feared that a sentence that could create problems would then be recorded, and so he left it at that. If Sensini appreciates this small courtesy, she doesn't show it.

"So you were at home at that time. Did you see anything? Anyone coming or going? Cars in the driveway or in the courtyard of the villa?"

No, he had seen nothing, nothing unusual, anyway. He couldn't swear he hadn't seen Carlos, because he came and went all the time and was part of the landscape, so to speak. But before the murder he was not in the habit of peeking into the courtyard...

Then he had to answer a thousand questions about his relationship with the widow Bastoni, with her late husband Cavalier Bastoni, about the purchase of the annex...Did Parrini visit the villa often?

"Never."

"Come on, you must have been invited now and again!"

"Yes, a couple of times, but years ago, when Cavalier Bastoni proposed the house deal to me. I couldn't refuse the invitation; he practically made me a gift of it..."

"So we won't find your fingerprints in there? Think carefully."

He was beginning to get annoyed. If all that playacting was aimed at getting his statements down on a sheet of paper, that's fine, he got that. But this was a bit too much.

"Am I suspected of something?"

"No, but your name suddenly appeared during the investigation, and we have to verify everything."

Appeared during the investigation. Okay, you've already said that, but in what way?

Meanwhile, after a light knock that had not waited for an answer, the tall deputy chief, whom Parrini had already seen together with Sensini, who had drunk coffee at his house, came into the room. The policeman, in plain clothes, greets him with a slight bow, of his head only, and waits. She motions to him to speak, he indicates Parrini with his eyes, as if to say: I'm to speak in front of him? She huffs and motions to him again.

"Come on, Zarli, out with it, fast, I've got stuff to do."

"The search of D'Onofrio's place, nothing to report. We also searched his car, there is something interesting there, I'll explain it better later, but in the meantime we have logged in some objects that we seized. They're over there, in a box, no big deal, but maybe you'll want to take a look at them."

"Yes, thank you."

But you can see that he has something else to add and that he's hesitating, so Sensini has a surge of irritation.

"Come on, Zarli, say what you have to say, don't worry, Maestro Parrini here is not under investigation and has only been summoned to sign his statement. Let's hear it!"

"We stopped Pinzago an hour ago, he was at the shop where his wife works, we informed him that he was being detained, he is waiting over there, in our office, he doesn't have a lawyer, they are looking for one, it will take a while."

"Well, thank you, tell them to hurry up, go ahead," said Sensini.

He turned on his heels and went out as discreetly as he had come in.

Now there is a pall of silence in the room and someone has to break it, so it's up to him.

"Can you tell me how I... how did you say it? Appeared during the investigation?"

"Yes, I can tell you, Parrini. You're named in the will of the widow Bastoni, two million euros."

"What?"

Surprise is a treacherous beast that assails you when you least expect it, transforms your face and opens your eyes wide, it's like a snakebite, and judging by Parrini's face and eyes, this is a big snake. In the will? Two million? He must have seen her a dozen times, the widow Bastoni, and all they had said to each other was good morning madam, good morning to you, sir, and maybe sometimes they had talked about the weather—he doesn't remember, but maybe. Ah, yes, and then once she kindly told him that if he wished, he could keep his car behind the villa, where she kept her old Mercedes, but he doesn't have a car, so he had thanked her and that was it.

End of the relationship. Rather scanty for two million euros.

Now Sensini turns to the cop behind the computer.

"Got everything?"

"Yes."

"Well, print two copies and prepare them to be signed. And leave us alone for a moment, please."

The policeman leaves, and finally Sensini seems to relax.

"Forgive me for the drama, Maestro, but we need the signed statement, and I wanted to give you the news about the will in person."

He is still stunned, his eyes have not yet returned to normal, the poison of surprise is entering into circulation.

"I advise you not to feel them already in your pocket, the two million, because there are two wills, one, the one that names you, has a note attached from the old Cavalier Bastoni with his last wishes, among which there is the legacy for you... he calls you the greatest artist that he had known, I might add... Then there is another one, but it is not filed with a notary and so we have to figure out whether it is valid, and all the long and complicated things that the lawyers will have to look into."

“I’m seventy-four,” laughs Manlio Parrini, “I don’t think I can deal with long and complicated things.” She shrugged, as if to say that was his problem and that she had enough of her own, but she put on an asshole smile.

“Technically, the appearance of this will makes you a suspect, Parrini.”

He laughed, openly, this time.

“Funny, but I don’t have the physique of the student from St. Petersburg, nor his tendency to remorse. I declare myself innocent, Your Honor.”

“Don’t worry, no one thinks you go around strangling old ladies, and then... Villa Bastoni, on the morning of the murder, was already too crowded, believe me, even without the famous director getting in the way.”

“That is?”

“Don’t presume to know too much, Parrini, I already have my problems...”

“I helped you, though!”

“Listen, we are sure that Furlan, the pissed-off auto electrician, was there that morning, he admitted it himself, so... Then there is Pinzago, who was there for sure, because he left from there to go shopping, he came back with the bags from the supermarket and found the corpse... He lied to us, by the way, so he’s been detained too, now we will hear what he has to say... Then we have some evidence that the poor grandnephew was also there, on the morning of the murder, the one the newspapers say is confused and in grief...”

"And then two strands of a woman's blond hair on the corpse."

"That's right. You understand that, for a murder scene, there were already too many people, if you had been there too it really would have been too much."

Manlio Parrini laughed again.

"What's there to laugh about?"

"It sounds like a Feydeau comedy, one enters, the other one leaves, the first one leaves and yet another enters, through doors, closets, secret passages."

There was a knock on the door and Sensini said, "Come in!" The policeman from before, the one who took the report, entered with a few sheets of paper in his hand, which he placed on Sensini's desk. She took a copy and offered Parrini a pen, he signed without even reading it.

Then they shook hands, and he went out, into those immense corridors with very high vaulted ceilings, cold, made to intimidate. No one accompanied him this time, he made it out to the sidewalk alone, lit a cigarette. Two million, not something to shake a stick at. Two million was not enough, of course, to produce the film on his own, but maybe for him to put his foot down, yes, to defend his screenwriter and to insist on the actor he wanted, not the American poster boy they were trying to impose on him.

But then, he said to himself, it was a very theoretical two million. If there is a battle of the wills, replete with the big shot's lawyers, appraisals, counterappraisals, probate courts . . . Anyway, standing on the sidewalk in front of the steps of the Palace of Justice, he cannot help but send a thought to the late Cavalier Bastoni, who had given him that surprise almost ten years after his death . . . Nice move, Cavalier!

"You were my guest for a lunch, so now you can buy me a cup of coffee. Eh, Maestro?"

Manlio Parrini turns abruptly, and finds himself looking at Claudio Tarsi, the reporter from the *Corriere*. He still has his light trench coat and his shoulder bag, the slappable face he can't change, of course, and he must have learned to wear it with a certain nonchalance.

"Good morning, Tarsi. As you know very well, I have nothing to say to you, but I would still like to congratulate you, I haven't read crime news for years, but your pieces I read." He said it with unexpected good humor, spontaneously. Then he thought, a little ashamed, that perhaps at the origin of that affability there were a couple of words that are always nice to hear. "Two million," for example.

They found seats at the tables in the bar in Corso di Porta Vittoria, almost halfway between the court and the Sormani library, where Parrini had done his research in the newspapers of the Fascist period.

"They've detained the handyman, too," said Tarsi. "The case is starting to become entertaining."

"Sensini doesn't think so."

"You tricked me, Maestro. You gave me fake news to create a trap... what's going on, are you working for the prosecutor's office? Sensini is sharp, she doesn't need any help, you know?"

"You're right, but I had no idea it was a trap, I told you the only thing I knew... And then it made it possible to detain the young grandnephew, didn't it?"

"A trap is a trap, who cares if it's for a good cause."

"Don't play the sophist, please."

"But yes, you're right, I was a jerk to fall for it... So, why this convocation?"

"Don't get too excited, it was just for me to sign my statement for the record... person informed of the facts. I'm actually not informed at all, but still... A formality, that's all."

"Yes, I think you are the least of Sensini's problems. She says she has some evidence that the grandnephew was also at the scene of the crime, he is an ace that she's keeping up her sleeve, but now the cards pass to the judge for the preliminary hearing, who has to validate the arrest, so if she really has an ace, she'll have to pull it out... You can keep criminals, fools, and poor people under arrest, but not the son of a big banker on a mission for the government, unless you have a royal flush."

"I don't know anything about it, there's no point in insisting."

"Yes, of course, I assure you that I am not trying to extort anything from you. Just remind you of our pact."

"We have no pact, as you know very well."

Parrini was impressed, however. Yes, he knew that one of the qualities of old reporters is perseverance, never giving up, he had met journalists, many years before. But he thought that those things had been lost a bit, and instead this one...

"In short, Sensini does not want to let him go, the young D'Onofrio, but the investigating judge will say other things. We'll see. There is still the woman." Tarsi sounded like someone who was thinking out loud.

"What woman?"

"The one whose hair was on the corpse."

"Ah, of course! *Cherchez la femme!*" laughed Manlio Parrini.

He felt more relieved, this snoop knew nothing about the will. Better that way, all he needed was to end up in the newspapers with inferences and winking half sentences.

"And even the butler, if we want to stick to the classics... What's his name... Pinzago, yes, Sensini must have had something new on him, otherwise she would have detained him earlier."

"She says he lied to her."

Parrini bites his tongue. Maybe he shouldn't have said it, in fact he certainly shouldn't. He realizes that from the small passing flash of light—less than a hundredth of a second—in Tarsi's eyes. Idiot!

"Oh, yes," says Tarsi. "Telling lies to a deputy prosecutor about a murder case, especially if you're the one who found the body, doesn't strike me as a good move."

His opinion got no response, it had floated a little under the branches of the trees of the avenue, it had wandered over the heads of lawyers, witnesses, defendants, sales clerks who came and went from the bar for midmorning coffee, and then it had dissolved, together with the fine particle dust.

Claudio Tarsi stood up, stretched out a hand, and took his leave with his slappable face, without even making the gesture of paying for the coffee. After all, this one was on him, right?

He watched him walk away with his disappointed bear step, but he didn't get up. Instead he picked up the phone and called Sara De Viesti.

"Well? Am I going to see you or not?"

"Yes, I thought I would come right after lunch."

"Okay, I'll wait for you at home... How are you coming?"

"Well, I was thinking by taxi."

"No, come by car if you can, I'll take you for a ride."

"Yes, master."

"You dummy."

He found himself with a couple of hours of free time, a beautiful day, with the sky opening up and now it was almost all blue. He starts down Via Cesare Battisti, the sidewalk in the shade, and walks to Largo Augusto, then slips almost without realizing it into Piazza Fontana. He enjoys the people passing by, some rushing to the registry office in Via Larga, some running quick errands, no one, it seems to him, walking aimlessly like him.

Of course, four people at the scene of the crime, within three, four hours, was quite an amazing thing, and it really reminded him of classic detective stories, including the ones by De Angelis. Several suspects and only one murderer. Commissioner De Vincenzi would have gathered them in a room, in the last or next-to-last chapter, and would have lined up his intuitions, some material evidence, and a lot of observation of the human soul, and he would have revealed the mystery.

> He did not believe in circumstantial evidence, any more than he believed in the certainty of proof. No piece of evidence was certain and all of them were. No criminal signs his crime. Chance signs it for him.*

Novels, of course, literary fiction, streetcar books. But Manlio Parrini was chuckling to himself.

He takes the metro in Piazza Duomo, surrounded by a swarm of Japanese tourists.

---

* Augusto De Angelis, *Six Women and a Book.*

14

IF SARA DE VIESTI IS SURPRISED, SHE DOESN'T SHOW IT.

She expects anything and everything from that crazy old man. She was anticipating an afternoon of study and discussion in the comfortable living area of the annex, and instead she found herself driving in the middle of traffic, with Manlio Parrini at her side, more chatty than usual. They haven't yet left Milan and he has already told her about the summons to the prosecutor's office, the signed statement, and—boom—the will and the two million euros from the widow Bastoni, drawn up in accordance with the Cavalier's last wishes.

"Great, you're rich, take me out for a proper dinner," she said.

She was driving with a certain expertise a rickety Fiat 500, all noise and vibration, that had trouble shifting into third. She wove in and out in the Milanese early afternoon traffic, and he talked, partly about the journalist from the *Corriere*, partly about the detention of Carlos the butler, and partly about the grandnephew of the dead widow. But it was all just a delaying tactic.

When they got on the highway, he decided to uncover the bucket of shit.

"They don't want you, they have to take you because I want you, but they strongly advise calling in another screenwriter to work with you, someone who won't make trouble and who's not a rabble-rouser like you."

He told her about the letter from the producer Luca Corrioni, about its arm-twisting contents, the American producers who were supposed to cofinance the film, and about the actor they had chosen, Steven Highner, and on hearing that name Sara De Viesti raised her eyes skyward, but she didn't say anything.

He continued, complaining some and swearing some but above all waiting for Sara to make a scene. But instead she was as cold and dry as a well-made martini.

"I expected as much, it's your fault...you figured your big name was enough. Manlio Parrini, the Maestro! And all of the doors would spring open, without any discussion, it would be the Red Sea on the arrival of Moses, who steps in behind the camera for the first time in thirty years...Things have changed, Manlio, that's not the way it works! To make a film at that level, today, the real screenwriter is called marketing, they do an audience survey, on what the audience wants, that is . . . on what they think it wants, it wouldn't surprise me if they had some kind of algorithm . . ."

"You know damn well that I don't give a fuck about 'that level,' as you call it. As far as I'm concerned it could even be an arthouse film that plays in ten theaters and a few festivals, as long as it is my film."

"Ah, the niche! And instead they want the platforms, a blockbuster, and to do that, it's not enough to have the Maestro of *Broken Truths*, let alone the . . . how did you put it? The rabble-rousing lady screenwriter? Yeah, I like that."

Then she looked at him, for a long instant. So long that he was afraid she was going to drive off the road, because in that stretch, after Merone, after Erba, the curves start coming fast and furious and it would be better . . .

"I don't want to impose any conditions, Manlio, and you know that I would like to do a film with you. But I don't want anyone imposing conditions on me either. If I had accepted compromises and dirty deals I wouldn't have a car that vibrates like a blender and a mortgage coming out of my ass. I'd rather go clean stairwells."

"That's why you're here today rather than a driver from StratoFilm with two assistants and a production secretary, you know?"

"Pact of steel?" she said. It sounded like a signature in blood.

"Pact of steel."

He meant to say it was that or nothing. Either the story of Augusto De Angelis would be like they wanted it to be, or they would both go back to their respective occupations, she to documentaries and experimental films, he back to his little house and maybe...maybe yes, it would be the right time for the dog and the bocce club. And it wasn't just because of the Americans, their algorithm and the beefcake actor, expressive as a bale of hay, no. It would be for other reasons, much more dense.

Because the story of De Angelis, as they had come to think of it, was a story of complete, perfect injustice. First the pressure tactics, the censorship, then the ever tighter inner circle, then the war, the brutality, the sequestering of books, then jail, then torture. It was not the biography of one man, it was the biography of a nation, and then also a metaphor for cultural work in this country. It was the whispering of "You can't do this," "It's not right," the dictatorship of "better not," to live in peace. Like in a 1930s detective story: an Italian murderer? Better a foreigner. The poetic police detective? Better muscular and brutal. Crime? That belongs to the Americans, the English, and the list could go on. No suicides, they're prohibited. No dialects, they're frowned upon. No seamy atmosphere, inappropriate. The list could go on for hours: the film they had in mind was a film about the lack of air, when the atmosphere becomes rarefied, of the shrinking of the space for freedom. The producer's letter seemed like confirmation that there was a great need for such a film.

Now, luckily, Sara De Viesti was looking at the road.

"You realize how similar that letter is, almost a photocopy, to the reader's opinion I sent you, don't you? De Angelis was told to make small changes, to adjust the tone, to attenuate the murkiness that was in his novels. So we're supposed to round out the corners, please the popcorn eaters in the multiplexes, right? It's more than a metaphor, Manlio, it's exactly the same thing."

She wasn't attacking him, but he still felt the need to defend himself.

"And why would I have called you otherwise? Sorry."

"Okay, right. So let's think about the film we want to make, and if it's a good idea, we'll also find someone who has the balls to produce it. Now let's get to work, come on, enough with the bullshit."

They started working, in their own way. They parked the car on the lakefront, and then walked slowly through Bellagio, up to the pier, letting themselves be captured by the context, by a panorama of rare beauty. Even though it is four in the afternoon and there is a wisp of sunshine, a small mist rises from the water that softens everything. They pass in front of beautiful villas, some so polished they look spanking new, others more wilted, and they are the most fascinating.

"Do you know that Bellagio was a kind of cultural capital? Everyone has passed through here, Manzoni, Stendhal, Flaubert...in the early twentieth century there were three theaters, and the most renowned hotels in Italy..."

In fact, the point is mind-blowing. The arrow of land that slips into Lake Como, which divides its two branches, culminates right there, in Bellagio. De Angelis had come there as an evacuee, with his family, his granddaughters, a kind of refuge far away from those who were looking for him...Not only him, there were a lot of people who had left Milan to take refuge in that magnificent place, thinking it would be a quiet area. And it was partly true, no one was bombing there, even if in 1944 the situation was not calm at all: the partisan bands were gaining strength, the Germans were afraid and becoming more ferocious, the Fascists of the Republic of Salò ruled with fear.

Manlio Parrini has to see it, that gloomy atmosphere, he must have it in his head before creating it with lights and shots. The pearl of the lake, the gem of the Belle Époque that had so many theaters, and cafés, and restaurants, had become a gloomy place where a wrong word could cost you dearly.

Arriving in front of San Giovanni, there is a small tourist port and the pier.

That's where Augusto De Angelis was beaten up, on July 2 of 1944.

Sara De Viesti is sitting on a bench, looking out at the lake, the sailboats, a boat that is docking on the opposite shore, in Tremezzo. The Maestro, on the other hand, is pacing back and forth, every now and then he bends down, or imagines narrow shots with his eyes, where to put the camera and the trolley for the sequence shot. He must see it in his head, the beating, the aggression. He imagines removing the sound, leaving only the gestures, allowing the violence of those blows to speak for itself, so that the viewer comes out somehow stunned, himself feeling bruised.

Then he goes back, sits on the bench, lights a cigarette.

She tells him how she has imagined the opening scene.

Augusto De Angelis, in his studio in Milan, is reading the suggestions that come to him from the publishing house, looking despondent, he riffles through the manuscript, you can see that he crosses out entire passages. The scene fades into another interior, more spartan, less bourgeois, the office of Inspector De Vincenzi, at the police headquarters in Piazza San Fedele. De Vincenzi answers the black phone. Dissolve. De Angelis is also on the phone now. He solicits a payment, explains the changes he is making to his book. Fade. A bourgeois interior, opulent, almost too opulent, perfectly lit, a top hat on the ground, a monocle with a broken lens, a corpse on the ground, and a coroner bent over the body.

"You are already into the story," says Sara De Viesti.

Manlio Parrini smiles. She is good, this girl. Huge pain in the ass, but good.

For dinner they end up in a local trattoria, just outside the town, after a few kilometers of ascending curves. At sunset, the view from there is breathtaking, the lake is as dark as night, the last rays of the sun cut white scratches on the water, they ask for a table outside even though a cold breeze is blowing. They immediately ask for wine, they will take care of ordering, they are not in a hurry. Sara De Viesti starts again with her theory.

"It's not a cold case, Manlio, we need to be clear about that."

"I've already told you how I feel."

She took out of her bag a sheet of paper, all quilted with notes, arrows, underlinings, question marks. An article in the *Corriere della Sera* dated October 1950. The title is passed over with a yellow highlighter.

THE NOVELIST AUGUSTO DE ANGELIS WAS PERSECUTED BUT NOT KILLED

> The investigations of the Magistracy exonerate one of his assailants from the charge of manslaughter*

"Persecuted but not killed, it's already bullshit," says Parrini.

"Shut up, listen here."

So she read the article. Pietro Varoni is acquitted by amnesty. Yes, he had assaulted Augusto De Angelis, on July 2, 1944, at the Bellagio pier. He was a fairly well-known Fascist in Milan, an evacuee on the lake, while De Angelis is said to have evacuated too, but "because he was politically persecuted."

Manlio Parrini listens with great attention. He feels that something will happen, that in that photocopy of an old and yellowed newspaper there is some detail that he will not like. And he also knows that what he will not like is the patch he is putting on the hole of a life that ended badly, trampled on, a patch on a ferocious injustice. There is a broken truth in those lines, he is sure, he could swear to it with his eyes closed.

She reads aloud:

> De Angelis considered Varoni to be the author of a complaint against him presented to the Nazi-Fascists, for having expressed pro-English sentiments and

* *Corriere della Sera*, Friday–Saturday, October 20–21, 1950. Historical archive of the *Corriere della Sera*. The article is not signed.

shouted "Long live England!" at the announcement of an Allied victory.

Manlio Parrini snorts. She continues reading:

This seems to have been the origin of a quarrel that arose between the two; a squabble that ended with some blows and, it seems, a kick that Varoni is believed to have delivered to the opponent. Shortly afterward, De Angelis, who was infirm and increasingly persecuted, found refuge in the hospital of Como, where he died "of lung disease," at least according to the doctors' report.

The wine is the house wine, a full-bodied and strong red, very good. So it is not because of the wine that Manlio Parrini makes a grumpy frown.

"Shortly after? The beating took place on July 2 and De Angelis died on July 18: two weeks of agony! And then . . . 'squabble'? You see that it doesn't hold up, don't you?"

"Will you shut up? Let me finish!"

The judicial authority, however, to which the Carabinieri had reported the quarrel, appropriately keeping silent about his political motive, ordered the exhumation of the body for a necropsy. And this

> established that the injuries caused to the novelist by Varoni had been "a contributing cause of death." Varoni was therefore arrested on charges of manslaughter, but was subsequently placed on provisional release.

"Fucking manslaughter!"

"Listen, Manlio, if you don't let me finish, I'll take it and leave, okay?"

In the meantime, the pizzoccheri had arrived, two huge dishes, full of that pasta that is not pasta, cheese, vegetables, all dripping, more than dripping, drenched in butter.

"Here, shut up and eat, let me finish, let the cholesterol take its course."

> In the meantime, at the request of the defense, Prof. Cazzaniga of the University of Milan was entrusted with a technical consultancy that denied that the cause of De Angelis's death could be traced back to Varoni's beatings.

Sara De Viesti looked up from the paper and looked at Maestro Parrini. She looked at him as if to say, see? Everything settled, two slaps and a squabble. Then she bowed her head again to read those very small characters mixed with ink.

Now, as has been said, the deputy prosecutor, in her indictment, believed that it should not be a question of manslaughter, but of simple voluntary injuries: hence the request for acquittal.

She put the paper on the table. Parrini said nothing, he continued to hunt for pizzoccheri in his huge plate, which was slowly emptying. He took another sip of wine and said:

"Eat, cold they're not nearly as good."

He had a paternal tone, as if he had escaped affection for that red-haired witch who now also drank wine and plunged her fork into that blessing, the highest culinary expression of Lombardy not in the Po Valley, food for mountain farmers.

The return trip was slower than the outward journey, more cautious, even if car speed, with De Viesti driving, was certainly not the main problem.

"If they stop us and give me an alcohol test, you'll come and visit me in San Vittore, right?"

"I'll be put in the same cell, if you want."

It was just a way to ease the tension, they both knew that they would discuss that 1950 article, that perhaps they would argue. Instead, he was working his way there slowly.

"You know there's another version, don't you?"

"And that would be?"

"Many biographies of De Angelis report it, but let's say that we trust the great OdB, Oreste del Buono, who among other things rediscovered and relaunched De Angelis's books at the beginning of the sixties... The alternative version says that a woman was involved."

"Explain."

"De Angelis walks along the lakefront, where we were today, and meets the woman who had denounced him. He has a spat with her, and here the versions differ. There are those who say that she apologized, she did not think that they would arrest him, she says she is sorry. Others say that he addressed her in a mean way, again because of the complaint she filed. There is also a somewhat absurd version that says that De Angelis had an affair with this woman... but I would forget about that, it seems fanciful to me. In short, Varoni was with this woman, he was her boyfriend, or a friend, we don't know, and at some point in the argument, he threw himself on De Angelis, brutally beating him."

This time, Sara De Viesti didn't take her eyes off the road, but spoke as if to herself.

"Do you like this version better?"

"It's not a question of whether I like it or not, even if the only convincing actress they propose is the one who would work for this part... I don't know if you know her, Irma Grotti."

"Yes, very good."

"Well, if I have to tell you the truth, I don't believe in one story or the other. I don't believe in an affair with a woman... come on, De Angelis was a man of the world, I don't see him looking for adventures in the place where he is evacuated... but I am sincere, even on the complaint of which the *Corriere* speaks. In short, he was a prominent character, from July 25 to September 8, 1943, he had also worked at the *Gazzetta del Popolo*, in that brief interlude in which the newspaper was almost free again... In short, he was not just any anti-Fascist, I don't see him in a bar shouting 'Long live England' like some factory worker on a break."

"Well, it was a complaint filed by a Fascist, nothing could be more likely than a lie."

"Of course, yes, of course. But there is a passage that interests me, in what you read earlier, when it says that the Carabinieri kept silent about the political matrix of the beating..."

"Well, you can understand if they had said that a Fascist had beaten an anti-Fascist, what's more, an intellectual, they might have given the assailant a medal."

"Good for you, brava, I'm interested in that carabiniere, the one who makes something up, even a woman, if necessary, even a question of horns, if necessary, so as not to let the aggressor get away with it..."

"Yes, it is an interesting passage. Meanwhile, thanks to the amnesty he was off the hook..."

"Of course. But don't you see that it is a cold case? Don't you see that everything is not clear and resolved?"

"No, Manlio. I see that there is a judgment, that the question has been closed, that the culprit was not judged to be guilty."

"Who fucking cares! There is an injustice, and justice was not done."

"Why, is justice ever done?"

The girl is disarming, yes, that's what he likes, but it can be irritating.

"You don't need to drive all the way to my place, leave me at a taxi stand."

She does, in fact, live on the other side of the city. They say goodbye on the fly at a traffic light, before it turns green.

15

PAGING THROUGH THE NEWSPAPERS, IN THE MORNING, has become a tired ritual. More than anything else, it helps him to eat his breakfast calmly. So he needs the newspapers to get down his first cup of coffee and he needs his first cup of coffee to digest the newspapers. Manlio Parrini realizes, a bit surprised, that he goes straight to the local news section, looking for the latest on the Bastoni crime. The thing has him hooked, even if, were he asked about it, he would deny it to his death. And there is plenty of news.

The preliminary hearing judge has validated the arrest of young D'Onofrio, against the predictions and wishes of his hotshot lawyers, who called a press conference to voice their complaints. They accused Deputy Prosecutor Sensini of being prejudiced and ill-disposed toward their client, a shaken and confused boy who did not commit any crime.

Neither the judge nor Sensini has responded, obviously, but that doesn't stop the old reliable Tarsi, in the *Corriere*, from chasing down the scuttlebutt behind the scenes. The chief prosecutor and Sensini have entered into open conflict. He insisted that she reformulate the charges, she stuck to her guns and even threw into her request for pretrial detention some other elements that had emerged from the investigation, and the judge had approved it. The repercussions of the friction at the highest levels of the prosecutor's office could be significant because there was already talk of a rush to judgment and some of the newspapers were raising suspicions that the confirmation of the detention order for young D'Onofrio was a subtle and indirect way to attack the government "while the father of the boy is conducting delicate monetary negotiations abroad."

Manlio Parrini lets out a little laugh, even the jerk who climbs over a wall to go and snoop on the scene of the crime becomes a political issue, what an absurd country. Anyway, it's clear that Sensini is under attack, and he's sorry to see that.

But, as usual, the one with the freshest news is Claudio Tarsi. Parrini imagines the web of relationships, contacts, conversations half spoken and half whispered in the bar of the Palace of Justice, or on the sidewalk of Via Freguglia, with lawyers, police investigators, clerks looking to use the press to their advantage. Talk about dirty work.

The domestic servant Carlos Manolo Pinzago has been detained and grilled in the prosecutor's office, where he was questioned for more than six hours before his detention was finally confirmed. Pinzago is currently in the Opera prison, the preliminary hearing judge will have to rule on him too in a few days. According to the *Corriere*, despite his lawyers' outcry, the position of the young D'Onofrio is getting more complicated, Sensini has pulled her aces out of her sleeve, even if it is not known exactly what those aces are. The hope is that someone will talk. The auto electrician Furlan, who—in another decision of the preliminary hearing judge, on a motion by his lawyer—has obtained house arrest, has been charged with theft and aiding and abetting in the case of murder, because he did not report the old woman's corpse, but he seems to have been cleared of the charge of strangling the widow Bastoni. That's something at least. In short, the case is very intricate.

Claudio Tarsi's big scoop, however, comes in the last lines of his piece, a whole page long. The reporter was able to read—he does not say how, obviously, Sensini will be furious—the report of the sequester of the murder scene at the villa. In addition to numerous folders of papers, documents, payment receipts, and various accounts, the shelves of seized materials in the prosecutor's office also held a box with a lot of money, more than four hundred thousand euros in cash. Meanwhile, Enrica Rigon, the maid, has been summoned for a new interrogation. The woman, who has been in the service of the Bastoni family for more than a decade, submitted to a DNA test without any problems, no arrest warrant has been issued for her, and she was questioned as a material witness. As was, Tarsi reports, the famous director Parrini, who reported to the prosecutor's office to sign his deposition and is—he adds maliciously—on excellent terms with the deputy prosecutor in charge of the investigation.

So, thanks to a line just thrown in there, Parrini is a friend of the cops, and he laughs again.

That's pretty much it. The other newspapers are in the chase, but they are several lengths behind. So they do what they can with the slippery art of inferences, two-bit moralistic pronouncements, to turn the intricate case into something that can be followed like a detective story. That's more than understandable, caught as they are between petty delinquency, muggings, and husbands who kill their wives, a case like this must seem to them like manna from heaven; too bad that the real news is in the hands of the other guy, who is a better journalist.

The rest of the pages Parrini peeks at with one eye, just the titles, and sometimes not even those. Domestic politics is the usual broken record, yet it occupies dozens of pages, sports he has no interest in. He takes a lackadaisical stroll through the entertainment section, and then suddenly freezes. A kind of paresis, a punch in the stomach, a sudden dizziness, like when a plane flies into an air pocket and seems about to crash.

ARE THE TRUTHS STILL BROKEN?
THE GREAT RETURN OF MANLIO PARRINI
The director of neo-neo-realism is said to be preparing a new film after his sensational and controversial exit from the industry almost thirty years ago
—Steven Highner: "Happy to work with a world-class maestro of cinema."

The article is as clear as mud. There is talk of "indiscretions," of "rumors," allusions to a detective story plot set in a historical period. A few dozen lines devoid of real content. The name of Sara De Viesti is not mentioned, no producers are named, nor is there anything about American capital, even if there's no doubt that's where it's coming from. Manlio Parrini reads the story and rereads it, with his anger mounting. He throws his iPad down on the couch and starts pacing up and down the living room of the annex, a caged tiger, a feline looking for someone to tear to pieces, growling at everyone and everything.

Then he decides, picks up the phone and calls StratoFilm.

A minute later the voice of Luca Corrioni is resonating in his ears, in a stupidly happy tone.

"Good morning, Parrini. Have you seen the front

page of the entertainment section in *La Stampa*? Things are starting to move!"

Disarming. So disarming that he's at a loss for words, to the extent that his silence alarms Corrioni, who thinks the line has gone dead.

"Hello? Parrini! Are you there?"

He threw it all out there as if he had taken a run-up, as though he had written down everything he wanted to say on a sheet of paper, and instead it's all anger and instinct. Yes, he knows that in certain cases you should think for a moment before you start talking, let off some steam, calm down. But what the fuck, he is Parrini, he doesn't need any filters to say what he thinks. So he says it.

"Rather than make a film with that nitwit Highner, I'd have one of my legs amputated, Corrioni. I want to know where this story came from. And it seems to me obvious that our relationship ends here."

To meet each other halfway, as reasonable people should do, first you need a way. But here what we've got is kilometers and kilometers of barren terrain, torturous, muddy. Even if Corrioni starts out cautiously.

"But why are you reacting like this? It's only a newspaper article, it creates expectation, curiosity. Highner is the actor of the moment, there are directors that would sell their mothers to..."

"I'm not one of those directors, Corrioni, my mother's been dead for forty years, I've got nothing to sell, and if I make a film, I'll make it the way I want to, with the actor that I choose…"

"But we can always decide that, Maestro, we'll decide, there's no obligation, nothing's been signed…for now it's good that there's some background noise, that people start talking about it…And to think that I had some good news to give you, I didn't expect this kind of reaction…Anyway, I'd like to see the screenplay, how far along are you and De Viesti? Oh, by the way, Franca Stranni has agreed to work alongside her, have you seen her series on Renato Carosone? Three episodes on Rai 1, great ratings, find it and take a look at it, Stranni will call you in a few days."

"That's supposed to be good news? Sounds like the results of a biopsy."

He had become sarcastic and wicked, but Corrioni had pretended not to hear. On the contrary, he just went on, making the situation worse, even if Parrini didn't believe it was possible things could get worse than that.

"Oh, plus, the Liguria Film Commission might be interested in the project, a nice chunk of money. All we need to do is shoot some scenes on the Riviera, Portofino would be ideal…That American market…"

"Sure, why not! The Portofino lakefront! And why not Las Vegas, Corrioni?"

He slammed the phone down in the face of that idiot. Stranni and her fucking biopics! Portofino. His anger might be blinding him, he didn't have a mirror and couldn't check, but his face was surely contorted in a ferocious grimace. He was right, but not now, no, thirty years ago, when he had thrown in the towel. He shouldn't have tried again, it made no sense, he couldn't stand to listen to this bullshit, it was humiliating.

Not even a minute to boil down, to take a deep breath, and the telephone rang. Not his cell, the landline, where nobody called unless it was to sell him subscriptions or new rates for electricity, gas, water, telephone, computer networks, pots and pans.

"Hello!"

An angelic voice:

"This is Alice Tornero, from *Vanity Fair*, may I speak to Maestro Parrini? We would like to do an interview on his return to the cinema, a photo shoot..."

"He's not in!"

He almost screamed. On the other end, an embarrassed and surprised silence.

"And do you know when I might find him?"

"No."

He slammed down the receiver with a violent gesture.

Then came the call from Sara De Viesti.

"It's me," she said, and nothing more.

It was one line that spoke volumes, which he understood immediately. It meant, "I saw the newspaper, what do you make of it? Have they trapped you? So it's decided? That expressionless American is going to be our De Angelis? You realize that in that case, I'll have nothing to do with it, don't you?"

Yes, it was all in that "It's me," and in the silence that followed.

Maybe this is how it should be done, thought Manlio Parrini. Don't scream, don't get venomous as a rattlesnake and stamp your feet and chew up the carpets. Maybe what was needed was that murderous coldness that Sara De Viesti has. Maybe it was enough to say: if that's the case, I won't be there. An observation, not a scene. Even in this situation, half irritating and half grotesque, he is surprised at his admiration for her. For her it was a magnificent opportunity to make a film with him, it was the leap from the underground to the big time, an opportunity to be seized at any cost. And instead, the girl kept her back straight, she did not intend to bend, she preferred to stick to her vulnerable integrity rather than come to terms. For a small fleeting moment, the stuff of a second, Manlio Parrini saw Augusto De Angelis, in his study, in front of a monumental typewriter, changing the names of his protagonists, changing Signor Bianchi into Mr. Brennan.

Sara would not have done that.

And what bothered him most: she believed that he, instead, would bend. So he ended up getting irritated with her too, the only one who didn't deserve it.

"We've already talked about it, Sara, either the film will be as we want it or there won't be any film at all. Is that clear?"

"You mean to tell me that shit in the newspaper came out without you knowing anything about it?"

So he had to tell her everything. Of the surprise of an hour earlier, when he had read that absurd article, and then also of the phone call with Corrioni, the reserve screenwriter, the Film Commission of Liguria… He was expecting irritation and anger, but instead she laughed. Fresh, sincere laughter that didn't contain even a drop of sarcasm, because there was no need.

"Strange that they didn't ask you to put a lesbian in the film, or an Asian, on the lakefront of Portofino. They do it, you know?"

She couldn't stop laughing, but then she suddenly became serious.

"Another false alarm, Manlio, it's always the same story. You believe in it, work on it, do research and study, and then…"

"And then what?"

"And then nothing comes of it."

"Nothing my ass, Sara. The more I hear of this bullshit, the more I get the urge to do it, this fucking movie. To do it in our way. I swear. And now that we may no longer have a producer, with the Americans and the potato-head in the starring role, we'll do it even better."

It sounded like a kind of challenge. And also like a promise.

They ended with the agreement to see each other the next day. She had gone ahead, now they had at least a draft of the script, but they would talk about it in person. They said goodbye with affection, she may not have been completely reassured, but enough not to disappear, the rest would come at their next meeting. Parrini felt determined and combative, he wasn't going to give up.

The landline phone rang again, twice. Three times. It seemed to him that it would never stop, but he didn't answer. Then his cell phone rang, and since he had it in his hand, he pressed the button and almost barked.

"Yes!"

"Don't you ever answer the phone, Maestro?"

Sensini.

"Good morning. Let's say it's a complicated day, but that will have to be enough for you because I'm quite upset and I don't want to treat you badly."

"I was wondering if you'd accept an invitation to dinner." Now he is amazed. He wasn't expecting this.

"Is it customary for a deputy prosecutor to invite to dinner a . . . shall we say, material witness?"

"No, Parrini, it's not at all customary, in fact it shouldn't be done for anything in the world, but please don't make things more difficult for me than they are."

“Okay, go for the dinner. Tonight? But you choose the restaurant.”

“Right, the restaurant. All we need is for us to be seen together in public... Come to my house, Parrini, I can’t guarantee you great food, but I assure you that the wine will be up to par.”

“And may I know why—”

She didn’t answer, she only gave him an address, Corso Vercelli 37, and the number to press on the intercom.

Now Manlio Parrini is striding through his living room again, making himself another coffee, in reality he would need a demijohn, and trying to get over the surprise. An invitation to dinner from the head of the investigation was truly an oddity. But why not? he tells himself, maybe it will distract him from his anger, discouragement, disappointment. The murder of the widow Bastoni was becoming a pastime, and playing Commissioner De Vincenzi could also be fun.

Outside it’s raining. He looks for a record on the shelf of vinyls and puts it on the turntable. He has not yet thought about the music of the film, and he will have to, because it is part of the lighting, the mood, the atmosphere. Now he has chosen side two of *Kind of Blue*, sometimes you need some certainty in life.

16

HE IS FEELING WORSE ALL THE TIME. FOR AT LEAST TEN days, he believes, if he has counted correctly, but he may be wrong, he has been in that bed, between life and death, with water in his lungs and perhaps even blood, because what he spits out is red and sticky.

And so he ended up practically clandestine. Out of money, out of work. The publishers he phoned, the ones for whom he had translated and edited novels and short stories, the ones to whom he had entrusted his novels, had turned to stone. Mute and unreachable. He could understand that: the wind had shifted to one direction, and then immediately back in the other direction again, and now, at least in the north of the country, anything was enough to send you to jail.

How had it been possible to survive on that inclined plane that was tilting more and more? Already in 1934 the Ministry had created the rule of sending three copies of each published book to the Prefecture. He had thought that it was nonsense, that none of those rather ignorant officials, put there perhaps because they knew how to carry the flag at the parade, had read very much. He wasn't the only one laughing.

Then things got more complicated and the squeeze got tighter. MinCulPop, with that absurd name, was established in 1937, in 1939 Pavolini arrived to direct it, it really couldn't have been any worse. And then further and further down: in July 1941 detective stories in installments and periodicals had been banned, and this was a hard blow, because he, between stories and translations, and advice to publishers, lived precisely on that. He still had the novels, but there was nothing to celebrate. A month later, in August, another crackdown: the Ministry decreed the seizure of a lot of previously published crime novels, a seizure that would affect the publishers. In addition, obstacles and boundary markers were set up, wrenches thrown into the works, harassment and abuse imposed: detective stories would be few and far between, like drops from a pipette, for publishers it would no longer be profitable, not at all. It was a good move for the regime. There was objective censorship "for reasons of a moral nature," but the most effective censorship came from the market: printing detective stories was no longer convenient, it was a losing proposition, and economically risky. In October

1941 he had closed the Mondadori series: the most famous detective stories, the ones whose yellow covers had become the color of the genre, were no longer available. For De Angelis, having a place in that series had been a goal, a culmination. He even remembers his chats with old man Mondadori, only a few years ago, but it seems like a century.

And then, with the war, came the blackouts, the bombing of cities, rationing, the filthy rot of war, and the glorious Empire falling apart, and our boys coming back on foot from Russia—those who made it back—how many of them still had any desire to read thrillers? Those books of entertainment and mystery intended to make their readers "lose their sleep"... How could they still be fascinating if readers were losing sleep over other, far more serious matters, including the fear of British bombs dropping on their heads?

The final end had come with two telegraph lines, a kind of epitaph, in June 1943:

> The Ministry of Popular Culture orders the seizure of all detective novels printed at any time and wherever offered for sale.*

In short, curtain. Lights out.

* Ordinance of the Ministry of Popular Culture, June 1, 1943.

His work was banned forever, his "Italian detective story," his dream of giving our own, national climate to a genre that the whole world read and appreciated, was wrecked by the most iron-fisted and obtuse prohibition. And to top it all off, he had thought he was witnessing a personal offense to himself, to his person, because his latest novel had come out that very April, gone from release to sequestered in a flash, not even the time to get on a bookstore shelf.*

All he could do was wander around. All that remained for him was to hide out, but how? Where? And now, now that he should find it ridiculous to think about these things while in all probability he is dying, dying like a beaten dog, he keeps on thinking of it as a personal offense, a snub directed right at him. A snub that had involved millions of people, the dead, the missing, the boys sent to the various fronts, those whom the Germans and the Fascists were now shooting in the streets, in the villages, even right around there... And he was worried about his streetcar novels? It was laughable, yes, but it was also evident that when you break the small truths, then you also break the big ones, that it starts with small deprivations, tiny prohibitions, and ends up massacring a people.

* The last novel by Augusto De Angelis, *Curti Bo and the Little Blond Tiger*, released at the end of April 1943 as part of the Sonzogno series, Detective and Mystery Novels.

• • •

He finds it increasingly difficult to stay awake, and perhaps this is a good thing. He no longer distinguishes delirium from lucid wakefulness, he wonders if it is already night, or if the sunlight in the ward is forcing him to close his eyes. He tries opening them to check. He can't, or maybe it's just pitch-dark.

17

HE FEELS LIKE AN IDIOT, THERE ON THE LANDING, WITH a tray of pastries in his hand, bought on the run in the first pastry shop he came across. As happens to everyone in these circumstances, he can't wait for her to open the door so he can say hello, put that stiff bundle in her hand, and get on with it, instead a man opens. Tall, athletic, in his sixties, the face of a sailor, with the wrinkles that the sun and the wind have sculpted in it. He introduces himself: Francesco. Then she arrives, Sensini, who completes the presentations. He is her husband.

The living room that also serves as a dining room is large and full of things, especially books, scattered here and there with a studied nonchalance that Parrini knows well, a disorder that decorates, that makes a house lived in, and lived in well, with means. A cocktail? Yes, of course yes, a pitcher arrives with some floating lemon slices. Gin and tonic.

So dinner was pleasant, even if he always had the feeling that there was more to it, the evening. And in fact, having served coffee in beautiful colored cups, her husband Francesco excused himself, he had some work to finish, he retired to his studio to see to it. He had to give a lecture the next day and had not yet finished preparing it. He had to compile the bibliography. A professor of law at the University of Milan, he had not said any more than this, and Parrini had not asked.

Instead, during dinner, they had talked about cinema, of course, about places to visit, about the holidays that had just ended before Sensini was overwhelmed by the investigations into the ongoing case, that of the widow Bastoni. A good bourgeois living room conversation, kind and calm, reassuring.

"Is it true that you are going back to make a film?" he had asked.

"Nonsense that the newspapers write," Parrini had replied, perhaps in a tone that implied "let's talk about something else, please."

And they had talked about something else, in fact. They were people of the world.

Then he and she remained, on a sofa, at a safe distance, a little turned toward each other, so that they could converse while looking at each other, but so that it did not seem like a conversation.

Someone has to start, however, and then he takes care of it.

"He's under pressure, isn't he?"

Chiara Sensini took her time, as if she were looking for a door through which to enter that chat for which she had summoned him, even if she had certainly already mulled over a lot about what to say to him.

"What do you say, Maestro? Nonsense that the newspapers print, right? But no, your friend Tarsi was right, there is friction in the prosecutor's office, this matter of the young D'Onofrio is bigger than it seemed initially. The thing cannot be hushed up, even the investigating judge had to confirm the arrest, even if the tide is rising...In a while the personal attacks will come, you know, the delegitimization that happens to all those who do delicate investigations...They've already begun."

"But apart from the lineage of the young man, what is delicate? That is, the accusations seem difficult to me to..."

They chatted amiably, of course, but Parrini had a tone that, underneath, asked: what do you want from me?

She walked around it a little longer, got up and took a couple of bottles, a cognac that looked like luxury and an ordinary whiskey, she placed them on the table full of books along with two glasses, but she neither served nor asked.

"In Matteo D'Onofrio's car there was a double bottom, not something improvised, just a hiding place built on purpose, practically undetectable."

"And you found it."

"By pure chance, believe me, or rather because of a mistake by the agents to whom we entrusted the search. The double bottom was controlled by the fog light switch, which they pressed by mistake with the ignition on. Pure chance."

Manlio Parrini smiles. Maybe she misinterprets his expression, but he is thinking of something else. You know what an obsession is, right? It's when you make everything, even what has nothing to do with it, square with your own fixed idea.

> Chance! All life is governed by Chance. You have to rely on it as an inevitable factor. The incident must be admitted as part of the base.*

"Drug business?" he asks.

"No, no drugs. The dogs didn't sniff out anything and even the analyses revealed no trace."

"So what then?"

"Come on, you can do it, Maestro!" This time she smiled. Then, since he didn't answer, she continued.

* Augusto De Angelis, "Lecture on the Detective Story."

"Money, Parrini. A lot of money. Old lady Bastoni had more than four hundred thousand euros at home, in a box. The boy, with that model girlfriend who lives in Basel, went up and down to Switzerland, often and willingly, as far as we know at least a couple of times a month. We asked for letters rogatory to see if he made substantial payments to any of his accounts, but it will take time."

"It's just an intuition, then."

"Well, well-founded intuition, though! Follow me. The night before the crime, the young D'Onofrio visits his aunt, but does not load the money from the black rents into the car, which in fact we found. Why?"

"You tell me."

"Yes, I'll tell you. The next morning Furlan, the auto electrician, must arrive with at least twenty thousand euros in cash—twenty-two thousand he says in the record—that is, the undeclared part of the one-year rent of his workshop. The old woman could not have known that he would not bring it, the money, indeed that he would go there to complain. Nothing could be easier than telling the nephew to come back the next morning, so as to make a full load."

"Yes, it stands, perhaps, but also not."

"And that's where Carlos comes in. He says he listened to the conversation and was sure that old Bastoni and her nephew had arranged to meet the next morning."

"Is that why you arrested him?"

"No, that's not why, Parrini. Because he falsified evidence, which in a murder case is a pretty serious matter."

Now, to be honest and frank, Manlio Parrini no longer understands anything. And, again for reasons of honesty and frankness, he does nothing to hide it. But he doesn't ask, he doesn't plead. It is evident that if Sensini has gone so far as to reveal office secrets to him that no one knows, she will not stop now. The question "What do you want from me?" has no answer at the moment, but you don't have to be in a hurry, in certain things, just wait and...

"The cups, Parrini. On the old woman's desk, in the study where the discussion with her nephew had taken place, and where she was killed the next morning, there were two cups with coffee residues, with the fingerprints of the lady and her nephew. We wondered if it was possible that in that tidy house, with the almost maniacal old lady, how it was possible that the cups of a coffee drunk at nine thirty the night before were still there at noon the next day."

"Aren't you exaggerating? The maid was in Veneto by the side of her dying mother, right? Maybe no one brought the cups into the kitchen."

She made the face of the cat that sees the mouse in a corner, and is already anticipating the leap.

"Of course, Parrini, of course. Too bad that on this point Carlos, the handyman butler, fell into contradiction, he got confused, in short. And do you know why? Because something didn't add up. The cup with the nephew's fingerprints was on the desk, yes, but in front of the old woman's chair, while the one with poor Mrs. Bastoni's fingerprints was opposite, in front of the guest's chair. Doesn't that seem strange to you?"

Now he is surprised. He never imagined it could be so much fun putting together the pieces of a murder investigation.

"Strange, yes, but not impossible."

"And here we have Pinzago's confession. In the end he caved, you know? We know how to do it even without raising our hands... His new version is that, when he returned around noon and found the woman dead, he was frightened, he was afraid that we would accuse him, the weak link, the foreign butler. Then he remembered that he had brought the two cups to the kitchen early that morning. Put them down on the counter by the sink, not washed, just removed from the desk in the study. He knew that the nephew would be coming by in the morning, indeed perhaps he thought that he had already come, perhaps that he had killed the woman. And so he went to the kitchen and took the cups and put them on the desk, as if to remove suspicion from himself and certify with false proof that someone else had been in the house while he was out shopping."

"Well, brilliant."

"Not very, Parrini, because, by bringing them back, he made a mistake in the position of the cups. So we do not know if the nephew, as he had said, but this is still according to Pinzago, really came by the villa on the morning of the crime, and on the other hand we know that Pinzago has altered the evidence, which makes him a first-class suspect, in addition to the fact that he was the last to see the widow Bastoni still alive."

"Well, you have a presumed culprit who was very unpresumed."

"Not exactly, Parrini, because I used those two cups to ask the preliminary judge to confirm the arrest of the young D'Onofrio. In short, I knew it was false evidence, but I pretended it was true so as not to release the boy. It's something they can use against me, especially those who want to take the investigation away from me and corroborate the theory that D'Onofrio was just up to some monkey business, 'a prank,' as they call it, to get inside the villa."

Now that question, the one from before, the one buzzing around like a troublesome fly, comes back more pressing than before. Why is she telling him all this? Why him? For what purpose? What does she want, in short? She was looking for a culprit, all right, she has one who's almost fried, Carlos the handyman, another just about to jump in the pan, the young grandnephew of the dead woman, and even a third, the more the merrier, the famous auto electrician.

What can the elderly director do to untangle such a knot? So he says it.

"Very interesting... instructive, in some ways... but what do you want from me?"

"I need a favor, Parrini."

In essence, the pressure was strong, the newspapers were not letting up, D'Onofrio's lawyers had appealed against the opinion of the preliminary judge and were threatening to raise hell, they are people who do not lack power. She had to get out the news of the double bottom in the boy's car, that detail had to leak out. Soon the lawyers would read Carlos's deposition, and his evidence of Matteo D'Onofrio's presence at the scene of the crime at an hour compatible with the murder would be shattered. The pressures would become unbearable, she would be crushed, and with her her investigation.

She asked him to do what he had already done, as a link with the press, to whisper some news to Claudio Tarsi of the *Corriere*. Only last time she had deceived him, and this time she hadn't. Only last time the news was false, and this time it wasn't.

Although the whole evening had been a succession of surprises and unanswered questions, this is the biggest surprise. Sensini must be reading that in his face, because she is staring at him like someone who has asked you for a courtesy and does not have the courage to say, "So?" but is thinking it with their whole self.

Manlio Parrini poured himself another finger of cognac. He wonders why he should do such a thing, but at the same time he also wonders why not. That Carlos had the strength, not only physical, to strangle the widow Bastoni he has no doubt, but isn't that perhaps the easiest, most painless solution? The frustrated domestic servant, perhaps harassed and humiliated by the greedy and stingy old usurer, and the nephew complicit in the shady affairs of his great-aunt who gets away with it, perhaps pocketing not only the legitimate inheritance, but also the Swiss accounts where the loot was deposited.

He wonders if his reflections have something to do with a sense of justice, or a misunderstood class consciousness, in which he finds himself in some way defending the poor, the loser, and complicating the life of the rich and fortunate scion.

What nonsense.

In reality, he is not saving anyone, apart from Sensini.

And on having this thought he asks himself again: why not?

Now he would like to ask a question, but he catches himself asking another:

"And the hair on the corpse?"

"This is a mystery, Parrini. It's not from the maid, the DNA speaks for itself. It would have been a good coup, even if we would have had to explain how she could have managed to return on the fly from Padua and return in record time, there are no compatible trains, that is . . . they're very tight. A car? Possible, but complicated. Of course, if the hair had been hers . . . but in short, no, nothing to do, the mystery remains."

Now he asks it, the question he wanted to ask before.

"What car does this Matteo D'Onofrio have?"

She understands that that question is a prelude to a yes, that he will play the game, that he has accepted her somewhat dirty proposal.

"A black Mercedes SUV."

She said it with a sense of relief.

Now they are saying goodbye. It is getting late. Sensini's husband has reappeared, just at the right moment, what timing, Parrini got the idea that he had somehow been eavesdropping to understand exactly when to return to the scene. And then, almost at the door, a sudden realization comes to him, an intuition, like a lightning strike. He tells himself no, no, what nonsense. And also: but how do you come up with this stuff, old fool? He calls himself an idiot, as people do when they've made a decision, but still reject it with a part of their brain. He was still fighting with himself when he got to the door.

"What if I asked you for a favor?" he said, putting on his jacket.

It was an impropriety. She couldn't fail to reciprocate, of course.

"If I may..."

So he explained to her, in a few words. Did the Carabinieri have a historical archive? And the court of Milan? What he needed were the details of an attack against Augusto De Angelis that took place on July 2, 1944, in Bellagio. The trial had ended in 1950, with the acquittal of the aggressor, Pietro Varoni, due to an amnesty. Were the minutes of the investigation or trial still lying around, in some hidden archive? Was it a thinkable thing or a simple fantasy of an old fool like himself?

Sensini made an astonished face—now it was her turn—but she returned to the living room and reappeared almost immediately with a pen in her hand, and wrote on a piece of paper the dates, the names, and what he had asked her.

"It seems highly unlikely to me, Parrini, something from as far back as 1944... but I promise to give it a try. You know what they say, don't you? If there is something to know, the Carabinieri know it. Give me a couple of days, but don't expect miracles."

The handshakes were hasty. They were not friends, everyone knew that. She had asked him for a favor, he had asked for another, however improbable, in return.

The dinner had been so-so, the cognac very good. The chat interesting.

Now it is not even midnight. Manlio Parrini is undecided whether to call a taxi or take a walk to Piazzale Baracca, where there is certainly a parking lot with white taxis waiting for customers. He decides to walk and in the meantime takes out his phone, and makes a call.

"It's late, am I waking you up?"

"Not at all, I'm working for you, things are coming out that we hadn't anticipated," says Sara De Viesti.

"Things are coming out in the middle of the night?"

"Online archives never sleep, Manlio, when you arrive in the twenty-first century, give me a whistle, I'll come and pick you up at the station."

"Well, tell me."

"No, tomorrow. Instead, you tell me. What is it, are you bored?" So he told her. Not of his mission as a spy on behalf of the deputy prosecutor, but of the small hopeless request he had made of her at the end of the evening. He didn't expect enthusiasm from Sara De Viesti, but neither did he expect it to flow by like a stream of cool water. And instead...

"We'll talk about it tomorrow," she concluded.

Fortunately, the taxi driver was not a talker, and Manlio Parrini was able to return home in a discreet silence, absorbed in thought.

18

HE HAD IMMERSED HIMSELF SO MUCH IN THE DETAILS of the mystery of Villa Bastoni that he had lost touch with his own reality. A depressing reality, to be honest, because the phone had never stopped ringing, and it was just ten in the morning. To begin with, two phone calls from important Italian newspapers: an editor of the entertainment section, announced by her secretary, and a film critic of medium importance, who acted like he was an old friend, citing authors and references that he thought he might like, in short, trying to seduce him, what nonsense.

They all want the same thing: an interview, an announcement, a confirmation. Is it true that you'll be working with Highner? Do you have an idea of when shooting will begin? What do you think of current cinema, now that you are back with a new film? He turned them away, polite but firm, saying that he was sorry about this huge misunderstanding triggered by one of their colleagues, but there was no film, Highner he had never even met, he couldn't figure out where that story came from, there was nothing to it.

The more he denied it, the more they became convinced that there was a film, that it was imminent, a matter of months.

The mystery remained of how they had his number, both his cell phone and his landline, and he was ready to bet that Luca Corrioni was trying to besiege him—or rather, to have him besieged—to exhaust him into submission.

So he unplugged the landline phone and made sure to look carefully at the display of the cell phone before answering, and then a longer than normal number appeared, a French area code.

"Monsieur Parrinì?"

Nathalie Bissieu had a hoarse and distant voice, very polite, without the cooing and babbling of a supplicant. She was a brilliant, highly cultured critic, who wrote little, for *Le Monde*, but when she wrote she was a Supreme Court. One of the few critics who was already active at the time of *Broken Truths* and had helped to construct its myth, had, so to speak, initiated its sanctification.

"Is it true, then, that you are finally going to make a new film?" Bissieu's Italian was what it was, half improvised and half scholastic, so he, out of courtesy, dusted off his French, and greeted her properly, an old-fashioned gentleman.

He explained to her that no, a film could not yet seriously be said to be in the works, that there was an idea under construction, but that the productive structure of European cinema did not guarantee him the freedom that he demanded and that therefore most likely...

Never, in all his life, had it crossed his mind to use the press as an instrument of pressure, to make people write something for his own benefit, or use and consumption. But now, sitting on the couch, or wandering around the house with the phone in his hand, he thought with a little corner of his brain that everyone did it. The producer Corrioni did it, Deputy Prosecutor Sensini did it, in short...

So, in half sentences, while Bissieu spoke without seeming to ask for information, he began to make small allusions. To make the film he wanted, a producer would be needed... Yes, it was a dense, complex film about the impossibility of being free, about the conditions, about the ties that prevent you from moving freely, about the supervised freedom of the intellectual, about his compromises, and about the undeniable fact that the lesser evil inevitably leads to the worst...

She did not ask impertinent or inappropriate questions. She didn't nag him for interviews or ask for revelations, on the contrary, they spoke with great tact and competence about cinema, the new filmmakers, the new currents, his abandonment, which had been, for those thirty years, an indictment of contemporary cinema. A good chat, almost an hour, in which Parrini dropped, without appearing to, some personal remarks: the dictatorship of big capital over screenplays, marketing that had replaced poetry. Then he said, in closing, that he was pleased with their chat, because the level was different, higher, truer, than the phone calls he was subjected to every minute. And she laughed.

"*Nous sommes deux vieux briscards,*" she joked. Two old veterans, two diehards.

It was true, he laughed too. And when she asked if she could publish that conversation—something that no one in Italy would have asked, they would have done it and that's it—he said yes, of course, as long as she did not announce films that did not yet exist, and did not name actors with the face of Iowa primary candidates.

She laughed again, not at the joke, but because she understood.

Now, having drunk his second cup of coffee, he is preparing his battle plan.

Sara De Viesti is coming right after lunch, with a draft of the script, complete, she says, even if only a first draft. It is the real work, finally, the one in which all the research converges, the one where the things to be told take shape, the lighting becomes precise, the scenes compose the complete framework.

How long had it been since he had done this? How long had he denied himself the magic of the composition of such a complex mosaic? For a small astonishing moment, Manlio Parrini realizes he is happy. An afternoon, perhaps an evening, the first of many afternoons and evenings, next to Sara, discussing shots and dialogues, bending the truth to make it seem more real. This was cinema, for him, and perhaps also for her, and they would think about money, marketing, the intricate logic of distribution, and the launch, all those matters that had nothing to do with cinema, later.

Now they had to build the weft, the fabric, organize the embroidery, weave everything like those artisans of Ouarzazate, or Isfahan, who make wonderful carpets starting from a few threads.

He puts his papers and notes on the table, dividing them by topic, by historical period. Here De Angelis's texts, about twenty books and printed booklets, there photocopies of the newspapers of the time, a couple of illustrated volumes on Milan in the early twentieth century… Like the chef who is setting the table, who wants everything perfect, neat and tidy for when the dishes arrive.

And the phone rings again.

"I understand that you don't like me, Maestro, but you're treating me really badly. We had a pact and then

I find in another newspaper that you are planning a film . . . I'm not one to be offended, but—"

Claudio Tarsi.

Manlio Parrini finds himself, unwittingly, with a mischievous smile on his face.

"If you are referring to that crap that came out yesterday, Tarsi, you're off the mark. What do you folks say? A hoax? That's what it is, a hoax."

"Your friend Sensini is in a bit of trouble, you know?"

"She's not my friend, I don't know what else I can say to convince you of that, and in any case she seems to me to be someone who knows how to get out of trouble on her own."

"You have nothing to say to me, then?"

"No, Tarsi, I have nothing to say to you, you are the best on the market, if you find the news yourself, even if . . ."

He left the sentence hanging, like those who, before casting the line with the hook attached, throw some food in the water to attract the fish. And the fish sniffed out the food.

"Why are you lying to me, Maestro, weren't we friends?"

"Your friend? Ah, that's all we need."

"All right, I'll buy you a coffee."

"I can't, Tarsi, normal people work, you know? I have stuff to do this afternoon, I don't have time for crime news."

"But I was saying now, in two minutes."

He thought he was ready for anything, but Tarsi had managed to amaze him.

"Why, where are you?"

"Outside your gate."

The man was the devil.

They settled on a bench in what the municipality of Milan, bless its heart, calls public green space. An island surrounded by traffic, with two benches, a pensioner with his dog, even one reading a paper newspaper, crazy stuff. Claudio Tarsi has his usual light trench coat, with a few stains, a shoulder bag, and a three-day beard. If it is possible to imagine an urban adventurer of the twenty-first century, well, he is it, out of place wherever he is, yet at ease everywhere. Manlio Parrini thinks he would be a good character for a film set in any era.

"You're right, Maestro, Sensini is someone who knows how to look out for herself, but this time the attack is concentric. There are the lawyers of the D'Onofrio family. Imagine, one of them was undersecretary of justice. Then there are the right-wing newspapers that shoot point-blank, you know what I mean... the judge looking to get himself in the limelight who takes aim at the VIP suspect to show off..."

"What bullshit."

"Yes, but bullshit, if you keep it up day after day... And then the chief prosecutor who can't stand her, who receives the minister's phone calls…And now this matter of false evidence. Sensini can no longer prove the presence of the young D'Onofrio at the scene of the crime at the time of the crime, Pinzago lied, probably to save his ass. The least she can do to get out of trouble is to formalize the charge of voluntary homicide against the butler and release the dead woman's nephew on lesser charges, breaking seals and trespassing, even though the domicile was a house from which he often came and went."

"Case solved, then."

"Maybe, but this does not improve Sensini's position, because there is nothing worse than saying that you have an ace up your sleeve, if that ace turns out to be a two of spades…These are things that they make you pay for, you know?"

"Sensini has other aces, Tarsi."

He said it as an afterthought, as if to himself, and he had cynically calculated it, that tone, that half voice, so that the other would raise his antennae. But Claudio Tarsi was too intelligent, or had seen too much, to beg for an indiscretion or ask directly, so he remained silent, playing defensively. And Parrini went on.

"But don't you find it strange that a twenty-six-year-old nephew goes so often to visit his grumpy old aunt? Affection is fine, but I mean…he had already gone the night before the murder, that's certain, and then he even climbed over a wall to go and poke around the next night. Okay, fine, so he was attached to his old great-aunt, but—"

"Inferences, Parrini. An ace has to be an ace, not the possibility that maybe, one day, it might be an ace."

"No doubt about it, but the feeling is that there was something more than affection between the nephew and the aunt, perhaps some business deal at stake..."

"More speculation."

"Of course, speculation. Or rather, fantasies of an old man who loves crime stories and who reads more and more into them because he is bored, but who knows how to put two and two together."

Tarsi says nothing, waiting.

"There were four hundred thousand euros in that house, weren't there? You wrote that."

"So what?"

"And then young D'Onofrio's beautiful car, which has been searched and is now under seizure, has a nice double bottom, very well hidden, a professional job, you know? You press a button on the dashboard and a spring pops in the back seat. If it weren't a latest model Mercedes, you could call it a treasure chest."

Claudio Tarsi's face has changed a bit. You can see that he is trying to remain impassive, but he can't quite manage it. He is taking in the information, and you can already see that he is pulling the strings, connecting the dots.

“The boy often goes to Switzerland, right?” adds Manlio Parrini. He has the air of someone who is saying: I feel sorry for you, I'll help you.

Now one of those noisy, gigantic, and shiny motorcycles, which should be in Arizona or Arkansas, not on a street in Milan, goes by. They let it sound off until the annoying rumble moves away.

“It might not be an ace, but it looks like a mighty good card,” says the journalist. But he immediately adds:

“And how do you know? Is this another trap like the last one? Did Sensini tell you to tell me to get herself out of trouble?”

Manlio Parrini made an offended face, even if he couldn't help laughing. He got up from the bench.

“I'm going to work, Tarsi, and if you want my advice, you should, too. Don't take the word of a bored old man, check the information you have, if you can, whether you publish it or not it's all the same to me, I don't work for Sensini, if that's what you mean, indeed, I don't work for anyone, not even for the cinema, at the moment, so...”

He left him there, seated and thoughtful, brooding over that chat, surrounded by the rodeo of cars that are going around the roundabout to get on the ring road, and he went on his way back home, to the villa of mysteries, to his papers and the industrious happiness that was waiting there for him, a carpet weaver racing toward his threads, his loom.

19

Scene 14. Exterior day.

Augusto De Angelis has an appointment in the Gallery. He is sitting at a table, at the restaurant Savini. To the waiter, who knows him, he says that he is waiting for someone, asks for a vermouth. He likes to sit and watch people go by. Then the person he was expecting arrives, he sits down. He is an elegant gentleman, with a walking stick.

"Three thousand lire," he says.

Augusto De Angelis grimaces. It's very little, he expected more.

"Yes, I know, but these are the figures, Augusto. The good news is that they would give you a contract for three novels, to be delivered within the year, all starring De Vincenzi. That's nine thousand, in the end, these days it's really not that bad, believe me."

"Three novels by the end of the year? It's June! Three books in six months? Who do you think I am?"

The other pretends not to hear.

"If you want my advice, make him a little more virile, your De Vincenzi. Psychology and intuitions are beautiful, Augusto, but against crime you also need a firm hand, a few punches, some interrogations, a little... well, toughness. The audience expects that."

"The public or the censors at the Ministry?"

"Well, I've said what I have to say, you do what you want, but the three thousand they'll give you only when the book is published, so if you want your novels to be rejected, think carefully."

He declines the offer of a drink, gets up, says goodbye, and disappears into the comings and goings of the Gallery, a minute and he is already gone.

Augusto De Angelis finishes his vermouth, leaves three lire on the table, and stands up too.

Change of light. Dissolve.

Scene 15. Interior night.

Augusto De Angelis is sitting at the typewriter. Dissolve.

Scene 16. Interior night.

Inspector De Vincenzi is questioning the maid.

"Did you touch anything?"

"Nothing, Inspector."

He bends over the corpse. Then he gets up and walks around the room, as if he were thinking of something else.

"We need to make the dissolves work well," says Manlio Parrini. "Setting off the two characters, De Angelis and De Vincenzi against each other in alternation, works, of course, but the changes of lighting must be . . . you know, not only fluid but ferocious."

"You're the boss," says Sara De Viesti.

They're holding sheets of paper, they take turns reading aloud, but she seems distracted, distant, there is something wrong. He's been pretending not to notice, so great was his desire to read, to see the scenes, to understand the tone, the lighting, to change everything, if necessary, but with a solid base from which to start. The happiness he was expecting, however, still hasn't materialized, because she has something gnawing at her, and he now knows her well enough to notice it.

"So, you want to talk?"

She didn't hold back.

"We're lying," she said. Then, to his astonished face, she got up and reached for her bag, took out a notebook and a printed sheet of paper.

"I have a friend who is doing a doctorate in Contemporary History, I asked him to rummage through some archives."

He puts down the papers and lights a cigarette. She continues.

"The central political archive has all the files of those arrested for anti-Fascism. Augusto De Angelis is not there."

Silence.

"It must be a mistake, Sara, a bureaucratic thing. The Germans took it, in the winter of '43, the situation was . . . confused, let's say."

"Or they arrested him for something else."

"He had just spent several months with the *Gazzetta del Popolo*, he was certainly on some blacklist of the regime."

She put down her notebook and picked up the other paper.

She read aloud:

THE WRITER
OF DETECTIVE NOVELS
AUGUSTO DE ANGELIS
CONVICTED OF FRAUD

Florence, February 14

A case against the well-known writer of crime novels Augusto De Angelis has ended at our Magistrate's Court. A few months ago, De Angelis had taken a room in one of the best hotels in Florence and, saying that

> he had large sums to collect, had postponed payments from day to day, creating a debt of 4642 lire. What's more, he had borrowed from the doormen of the same hotel 10.000 lire. Then the writer disappeared. De Angelis, judged in absentia, was sentenced to 18 months in prison with the aggravating circumstance of recidivism, because it seems that this is not the first of the "gimmicks" devised by the famous novelist.*

Manlio Parrini picks up the paper that Sara put down on the table. She has put her bent leg back under her ass and is looking at him. The news of De Angelis's conviction is a brief chronicle, alongside the *appointment of the new prefectural commissioners* and the *munificent gesture of a Roman engineer in favor of the Opera Balilla*. The rest is propaganda, a bit ridiculous, knowing now how things actually went: *The Anglo-Saxon war machine suffering continuous losses on the Italian front*. In other words, they were tooting their own horn and singing along with it too in February 1944, but that report from the front was as false as a thirty euro bill.

"This changes a few things," says Sara. "Don't you think?"

"In what sense?"

"Well, the popular version of the anti-Fascist De Angelis, arrested for anti-Fascism, is starting to sound a

* *La Gazzetta del Popolo*, February 14, 1944.

bit weak, what do you say? Someone who leaves without paying the bill at the Grand Hotel, who even borrows ten thousand lire... I remind you that in '44 an average salary was fifteen hundred or two thousand lire, tops, so ten thousand lire was a good sum."

"Sure, it's obvious, he was running away! He didn't know where to go, where to hide. A good hotel in Florence, why not? And you need money to keep hiding, what's strange?"

"What's strange is that we have to say it, Manlio, that the story is more complicated, that the profile changes."

"Nothing's changed, on the contrary, it's even better! It's all more real, it's more credible!"

He got up from the sofa and started walking around, slow steps, between the living room and the kitchen, then toward the large windows overlooking the courtyard, then back toward the sofas.

"Fucking think about it! A solid citizen, one who can take a hit, who plays along. Not entirely, not enough, you might say, judging from the pressure he's put under, from the censorship he's subjected to, but in essence an intellectual who does not flee to France, who does not join the partisans in the mountains. He wants to live, Sara, write his books. And that is no longer possible."

He is a river in flood now, maybe he's not even talking to her, but to himself.

"He tried in every way, of two minds, you could say, torn. On the one hand, the novelist who wants to write his novels, and on the other, the theorist of the Italian detective story who contests the regime's theses, not only on that subject, but in general... Maybe he had believed in it, in the fall of fascism, the months at the *Gazzetta del Popolo* would confirm that, he had exposed himself. But then... So, go, flee, hide, live by expedients... Swindle? Why not? He was looking for an escape hatch, a way out! Don't you see, Sara, the Italy of 1944? A strangled, airless country that is suffocating. With newspapers saying that the Americans are on the ropes in Sicily, in dire straits after the landing at Anzio. A continuous lie, a fetid air... And him? He is someone who wanted to do theater, almost rich at a certain point, one who had married well, his Amelia, one of the four Maggioni sisters, who grew up in luxury and led sheltered lives, a guy who aspired to salons, to the Milanese cultural scene. Who instead runs away like a thief... Do you see the story? Do you see it?"

He was almost screaming, but not at her. She had brought a revelation with her that should have put him in crisis and instead that revelation strengthened his vision. And he went on, fervent, finally convinced.

"It's not just the heroes that we're sorry for, Sara. It's for everyone else, the crushed, the humiliated, who wanted nothing more than to live in peace, eat, sleep, raise their children in a decent place, write detective stories and theatrical comedies! Bet on the horses, read French or English books. Fucking life!"

Sara De Viesti looks at him with a smile. To tell the truth, it's more in her eyes than on her lips.

That's him, the Maestro. That's him, Manlio Parrini at his best. Ferocious, straight as a spindle. She brought him that hitch, that ripple of history, and he knew how to read from the right point of view, he knew how to right wrongs, how to put broken truths back together again. Now she no longer had that uncertainty of before, that fear, those dark afterthoughts. Now, circumfused by her crown of red hair, she knew that the film was going to be made, that it would come out the way they wanted it, that a producer would be found somewhere, it didn't even seem like a problem anymore.

She would like to hug him, but it is not in her nature. Instead, she sits down and looks at him.

Manlio Parrini is back on the sofa, he has picked up the sheets again, this time with an energy that's denser, contagious, that he didn't have before.

"Let's move on," he said. She picked up the papers too.

Now her smile has even spread to her lips.

Scene 48. Interior day.

Editorial office of a newspaper, excited voices, desks full of papers, people coming and going.

Augusto De Angelis, at his desk, reading the papers that a courier brings him, reads them aloud. We can hear his words. The camera goes around the rooms, there is a feverish atmosphere.

Voice of De Angelis:

"Alarm at 0.35 . . . Ticinese neighborhood hit. Garibaldi neighborhood hit . . . Palazzo Marino severely damaged . . . Statues of the Cathedral fallen on the churchyard . . . The roads are cleared for the evacuation of the population . . . the Last Supper was saved, thanks be to God . . . Santa Maria delle Grazie damaged . . . Piazza San Fedele seriously affected . . . the central police headquarters destroyed . . ."

Dissolve.

Inspector De Vincenzi enters the police headquarters in Piazza San Fedele, greets the on-duty officer, and enters his bare and damp room. Sits down. He opens a drawer and takes out a book, he starts reading.

Audio.

Airplane engines, whistles, explosions. Dissolve.

Audio.

Telephones, typewriters, excited voices in the background.

Augusto De Angelis has stopped talking. He is staring at one of the papers they've brought him.

(Murmurs) "Everything is burning. In Milan, everything is burning."

Manlio Parrini looks up from the paper and looks at Sara De Viesti.

"We have to work on the sounds," he said.

"We have to work on everything," she replied.

The happiness he was expecting before, the expectation of a job well done, is all there now. Manlio Parrini, the Maestro, feels it descending on him, a state of quiet excitement.

They decide to take a break, have a drink. But she gets up, goes to the kitchen in search of alcohol while he clicks on his phone. A message.

It's Sensini, the message just says: "Thank you."

Now he is in front of his computer, the home page of the *Corriere* open, the cursor wanders here and there, then finds the title, it is the third story, tagged "Exclusive."

BASTONI CASE, TURN OF THE SCREW
FOR D'ONOFRIO

The text, which Parrini scrolls quickly, tells of the double bottom in the boy's car, of the suspicion that his trips to Switzerland were not only visits to his model girlfriend, that Matteo D'Onofrio's lawyers responded to the news with a laconic "No comment, let's wait for the papers." Deputy Prosecutor Sensini did not comment. Then other things to fill the space.

Sara De Viesti brought two glasses.

"I made them with vodka, the gin is finished."

"That's fine," he said. "No, even better."

20

THE CASE OF THE WIDOW BASTONI WAS SLUMBERING. No new wrinkles, and three days had passed since the scoop of the *Corriere*. Maybe the pressure on Chiara Sensini had eased a little, the rumors about a plot against the young D'Onofrio had decreased in intensity, the boy's lawyers were waiting with little hope for the outcome of their appeal of the detention order, they were still asking for his release, but without the tones of an attack on personal freedom. Letters rogatory had probably been sent to Switzerland, in search of bank accounts. Claudio Tarsi had not written for days and had not been in contact. Manlio Parrini's browsing through the morning newspapers had become, if possible, even faster. All quiet.

But there had been the fiery phone call from Luca Corrioni.

"Is this how you stab me in the back?" he said. In his anger he had switched to the informal *tu* form. He had read *Le Monde*.

THE TRUTHS ARE STILL BROKEN
NO ONE IN ITALY WANTS TO PRODUCE
THE NEW FILM BY MANLIO PARRINI

In effect, it was a low blow, because Parrini had wavered a bit between saying and not saying, but Bissieu had come down hard, adding to the things he had said, very few citations in quotation marks, her own considerations as an inveterate fan. The undue influence of producers, the ultimatums on the cast, the overwhelming power of two or three global players over film production, which mortified quality. In short, the Maestro also had his broken freedoms. Is it possible that in Italy no one wanted to invest in a sure masterpiece, in the return of the best living filmmaker? And if today a new Antonioni, a new De Sica, a new Pasolini were born on the peninsula, would he be forced to shoot petty bourgeois comedies or bloody thrillers full of special effects?

She had exaggerated a little, all right, but Manlio Parrini, in all honesty, had nodded at every line.

This time he was the one who phoned Bissieu, to thank her, receiving in return another long chat. A

French producer? Who knows, who knows, her article had stirred the waters by sparking a debate among the French cinephiles...

On the other hand, the annex of Villa Bastoni had become a seaport. In addition to Sara De Viesti there were other guests. Ferdinando Scotti, a young man of thirty-five, bearded, massive, arrived every morning with his beat-up motorcycle that smoked like a coal-fired power plant. He was the director of photography for whom Sara had advocated, a young genius at lighting. Manlio Parrini had seen some of his work, down in the tiny cinema room, and had found him a daredevil, someone convinced that light is part of the film just like the story and the framing; he thought so too. Scotti spent two days in an armchair, without saying a thing, reading the script word for word.

Then, one rainy and gloomy afternoon, Giovanna Marras, whom Parrini had met years earlier, also joined the group. Set designer, interior designer, costume designer. In short, she was the one who had to dress the film. An enormous and kind woman, in her fifties. She too, though she was the last to arrive, read through everything, asked questions, tried to make her way into the story of Augusto De Angelis, on tiptoe, but amused and enthusiastic.

Parrini looked around his living room and had the wonderful feeling of finally being in a collective. The meetings happened on the fly, with everyone in the same room all he had had to say was "Come here!" or "Meeting!" and everyone became attentive. What they wanted was a sliding of the story toward and into darkness, the death by beating of the protagonist. Slowly, inexorably, everything had to frazzle, fester, fray just as De Angelis's life had done, and as the country had done: a descent into hell, slow, almost imperceptible, almost subliminal. From the thirties, still bright and worldly, with the detective stories of De Angelis, the slender young ladies, the fat cats of upper-middle-class Milan, the glittering interiors of Art Nouveau and polished wood, things degraded into darker, shabbier settings, everything became poorer.

Young Scotti understood, he was the one who suggested the imperceptible variation of the lighting. Marras always had a huge sketchpad in her hand, and with two or three lines she translated their reflections into clothes, details, or sets. The Milan of 1935, 1936, the glittering international city where De Angelis placed as pawns his Mr. Brennans and his Miss O'Reallys, was not the Milan of 1943, or '44, frightened and scarred by English bombs, terrorized by the German command. That difference had to be seen in every detail, in the lighting, in the shades of gray, in the clothes, in the sparkling chandeliers turning into murky lamplight, because of the blackouts, sure, but also because of the decline, the fear, the imminent end.

• • •

Was Manlio Parrini happy? Yes, without a doubt. He felt alive and agitated, but above all he felt the responsibility of his work collective on his shoulders. What if no one came forward to produce the film? What if all that array of talent, ideas, suggestions, remained on paper? He swung between various moods. Maybe blowing off a rich and powerful production company like StratoFilm in that way had been stupid. Or maybe not. Maybe a big name in French cinema would come forward, one of those coproductions...

He shook his head to chase away the thought. It was necessary to redesign scene 65, or to think more deeply about sounds and music.

Saverio Protti, the actor, had also shown up for a couple of hours, the one Parrini imagined to be the perfect protagonist of the film, his De Angelis. Shy and reserved, honored to be summoned by the Maestro to have a chat. He was playing in a Chekhov piece, for another month, between Rome and Florence, and then he had contacts for a small production in Austria, but certainly a film by Parrini would have absolute priority. He listened to the story and was very surprised to learn that the father of the Italian detective story had ended up killed like a dog by the Fascists. Why was the story so little known? Why had such a historical metaphor been hidden? He left hopeful, excited, maybe he too had understood that that collective emanated something special. Probably, just after he left, he would run to the bookstore to get some detective stories from the thirties.

And then one evening, when the collective had disbanded, Sara had returned home, and the young Scotti had smoked up the neighborhood with his motorcycle, Chiara Sensini, the deputy prosecutor, called. Parrini could almost see her, in her living room, with her tanned husband, tired after a long day.

"I keep my promises, Maestro!" she said.

They didn't talk about the investigation, he asked why there was silence around the Bastoni case, and she glossed over it with a "We are working on it" that meant: let's talk about something else, if you don't mind.

"I have entrusted your research to a boy who works here, at the court. He's a little archive rat, don't ask me more, but in short, he might have something to tell you..."

Manlio Parrini went to sleep with the feeling that the threads were coming together, that there would not be one left out, that he would not have to revise the whole design, only small details, yes, of course, a million small details, but...

At a quarter past nine, with the city still humid but awash in glorious sunlight that colored it an intense yellow, Sara De Viesti arrived at the bar in Corso di Porta

Vittoria, next to the Palace of Justice, arousing a certain admiration among the lawyerly fauna. Her red hair was shining bright, and she stood straight and proud like a tawny coated horse, sure to win the Grand Prix. Feeling a little ridiculous, Manlio Parrini felt a little tremor as he moved toward her: something that every man present would have wanted to do in his place.

Delusions of grandeur, he thought, and he laughed at himself.

Alessandro Sacconi introduced himself with a big smile and a firm handshake. They were expecting a small and gray guy, dusty like his archives, and instead they were confronted with a young man not even thirty years old, with a Nirvana T-shirt, smashed sneakers, and a curious face, with the hair of a Led Zeppelin guitarist. He didn't take them to an office, as they expected he would, actually he doesn't have an office, he said. Then they walked corridors with the public, and then corridors without the public, and then internal stairs, illuminated with yellow bulbs, like an Albanian fallout shelter. Then one door, and then another, to the basement, so it seemed, where they found themselves in a cathedral with very high vaults, sheet metal hulls full of folders, binders, yellow envelopes, dust, light bulbs nearly exhausted from doing their work, others surrendered, burned out. Sacconi wandered seemingly randomly through the corridors, but he knew where to go. He took out a ladder, climbed up, and handed them, who were standing below, two huge heaps of paper tied by rubber bands gone limp with time. Then he leaned on a desk that was a few yards away and searched in those bundles of old papers, full of past lives, judgments, transcripts, yellowed photocopies, sheets of paper that seemed to crumble in his hands.

"There," he said, pulling an envelope out of all that chaos of paperwork. On the envelope there were numbers, dates, stamps, and a name: Varoni Pietro. The man who murdered De Angelis, the Fascist thug who threw those deadly punches and kicks at him on July 2, 1944.

"You have to look at it here," the boy said. "You don't take anything away, and no photocopies, take your time, I'll be back in a bit." Sara De Viesti looked for a chair, there was one already there, and opened her notebook. Manlio Parrini began leafing through the papers, his hands were shaking a little, for some reason he hoped she wouldn't notice.

There wasn't much to discover, though. The reconstruction of the *Corriere* from 1950 that Sara had brought him at the start of her investigation was perfect: Varoni had been definitively acquitted of the charge of manslaughter, thanks to the forensic reports, the good lawyers he had procured, and the desire to close a historical period that was uncomfortable for all concerned; for the victims, of course, but above all for the executioners. The charge had been downgraded to "voluntary injuries," nothing serious, the amnesty had done the rest. Manlio Parrini took a look at the defense lawyer's closing argument, where the term "squabble" recurs several times, the same used by the *Corriere* in its chronicle of the time. But all this is not interesting, they already know that. What they are looking for is something else, that is, the beginning of the story, the denunciation of the event, a report, a sheet, a deposition dating back to July 1944. So they go back with the dossier, skip the very complicated technical analyses, the pages written by the doctors, the results of the forensic tests after the corpse of De Angelis had been exhumed.

And then they find it. It is a yellowed, old sheet, typewritten with slightly skewed lines, the date is July 3, 1944 / Year XXII of the Regime.

> In the early afternoon of 2 July 1944 /XXII the local lieutenant of the Royal Carabinieri responded to a report of a scuffle from a passerby, in the locality of San Giovanni, Bellagio, at the pier...

No more than thirty lines, written in the language of the time that was flowery and convoluted at the same time. The victim of the beating, later identified as De Angelis Augusto, born in Rome on 28/06/1888 was transferred to the hospital in Como in a state of semi-consciousness. According to what was reconstructed by the Carabinieri, De Angelis had supposedly addressed a woman, in heated tones, a quarrel had arisen. The woman was accompanied by a man, who later turned out to be Pietro Varoni, who, with two friends who promptly intervened in his support, had allegedly beaten the victim for a long time, leaving him unconscious. The woman and the other two men, the accomplices of the beating, ran off without a trace and never reappear, neither in the subsequent reports, nor in the interrogations of Varoni, who always sustained the thesis of the "quarrel."

The report ends with the arrest of Varoni. No witnesses are cited. It is signed by Major Stefano Astarita, with repeated dates and stamps.

"Strange, isn't it?" says Sara De Viesti.

Manlio Parrini doesn't speak, he's envisioning the scene, he's turning on the light...in the early afternoon...He is thinking about where to put the camera, the sequence shot.

"That is," she continues, "everything stems from the argument with a woman, but the woman disappears, she is no longer there, neither in the police report nor in the transcript of the trial, not even her name, the same for her accomplices. Apparently, no one even asked Varoni who the lady was..."

Yes, strange.

• • •

When they go out into the light of day, they know as much as before, it's another fragmented, threadbare truth, which does not dissolve their doubts, which does not completely resolve the final scene of the film.

Their report to the collective, therefore, contains a bit of disappointment. Only Ferdinando Scotti gets a little agitated. The Carabinieri . . . in Bellagio, in the summer of 1944? The police report, which Sara De Viesti had photographed with her phone, spoke clearly, but . . .

So Sara summoned her longtime friend, the one with a doctorate who had already rummaged through the archives and political records for them. He arrived not even an hour later and, although excited by the presence of Manlio Parrini, the legend of cinema, he only had eyes for her. A funny scene. So the "De Angelis collective," as they jokingly called it, had expanded, now there was also an expert of the period, why hadn't they thought of that before? They dined—Chinese, this time—and talked freely, but above all they listened to this Gianni, who presided over a short lesson, looking furtively the whole time at Sara's red hair, with her maybe noticing his attention and maybe not, in any case she didn't show it.

No, of course, 1944 was not an easy year, if you were a carabiniere in Italy. In Rome, already in October 1943, the Carabinieri Corps had been disbanded, thousands of soldiers deported, or taken prisoner, some, indeed quite a few, had ended up among the ranks of the partisans, with the monarchists, precisely what the Germans wanted to avoid. In the north, in the Republic of Salò, the Carabinieri were officially still standing, with public security functions. In short, the Nazis and the militia were responsible for repressing the population, and they, the few Carabinieri still in service, were only supposed to catch the criminals and maintain public order. This is on paper. In reality, it happened that they collaborated with the Germans and Fascists for roundups of anti-Fascists and Jews, but mostly they went AWOL, simply by hiding out, or they went to fight with the partisan brigades.

"I should check the dates," says the young lovestruck historian, "but I believe that the Carabinieri Corps, in the north, was officially disbanded by the Germans at the beginning of August 1944. The Germans feared their loyalty to the king, and they were right. When they were disbanded, they were replaced by the National Republican Guard, a corps under the direct orders of Mussolini, who thought of them as modeled on the German SS. No one gave a damn anymore about criminals and public safety, the enemies were only the partisans and the civilians who helped them."

Theoretically, therefore, that report of the major of the Royal Carabinieri Stefano Astarita could have been a kind of last act of the Bellagio Carabinieri post, before deportation or escape.

"It would be nice to find him," says Sara De Viesti. "That is, not him, of course, but maybe a son, a grandson..."

"Tough one," replies the young historian. "I don't even know which archive to look in." He speaks with death in his heart, it is obvious, because he would go with that woman to look for anything anywhere.

Later, Parrini and Scotti locked themselves in the cinema room, the director of photography wanted the Maestro to see some effects, some filters that he used in a certain way. The collective had disbanded, as it did every night, aware that there was a lot of work to do, and that they were doing it in the dark, without knowing if the fruit of those efforts would one day really be screened in a movie theater. It was frustrating, yes, but none of them was going to give up now.

21

HE CAN'T SEE ANYMORE. IF THERE IS LIGHT HE HAS TO close his eyes, if it is dark he can keep them open, but the result is the same. The only hours of peace are the ones following the shot, then the pain subsides, even if his breathing remains labored. He feels his strength draining away.

Only his sense of hearing keeps him hooked to the world, at times he feels as if he's using his ears like fingernails, to cling to life, to sense that he is not alone in the world, with that whistling in his lungs. He feels like he's listening secretly to Radio London. The doctors buzzing around there are commenting on the events of the day, he understands and does not understand, struggles to isolate their sentences from the indistinct noise. The Americans are slow, very slow, it seems they'll never arrive. The Germans are becoming more frightened with each passing day, therefore more ferocious. There have been shootings, in Como, people are terrified, crushed by the terror of being touched even by suspicion.

At his bedside, but he could not swear it, that the major of the Carabinieri who had already visited him once has returned. He thinks he knows it for sure because to the question—"Can he understand me?"—that he had asked the nun, she had answered: "Only at times, but by now..."

Perhaps he had found a chair to sit next to him for a few minutes, had taken his hand, and had talked a little, more to himself than to that half corpse as white as a sheet, panting, more dead than alive.

"I did what I could," said the major.

"Your aggressor has been detained, but what's happening with law enforcement these days I can't tell you... I'm going away myself, and in a few days they're going to start rounding us up and sending us off to Germany, guilty of loyalty to our king."

In short, Augusto De Angelis, almost completely unconscious, had had, in his bed at the Sant'Anna hospital in Como, the precise sensation that not only was he dying, but that everything was dying. Everything was collapsing, it was all coming apart, everything he had seen and loved was no longer there. Now even that monarchist carabiniere, a monarchist like himself, was surrendering to greater things, to destiny.

He found himself thinking about it, that night, hoping that he would be able to save himself somehow. Switzerland is close, perhaps a carabiniere knows the right paths. Maybe.

Darkness enveloped him, but whether it was the darkness of the day or night he couldn't tell.

22

SATURDAY WAS A FREE DAY, AND SUNDAY TOO. THEY had decided that there was no hurry, but above all that the work completed had to settle a bit, writing seems different if you pick it up again after a break. So Manlio Parrini has nothing to do but confess to himself that that interval is weighing on him, that he is happy only when his house is resounding with voices, when opinions are being exchanged, variations suggested, when they are envisioning framings or interrelationships they hadn't thought of before.

Unannounced, Nathalie Bissieu phoned again, evidently she had taken to heart the matter of Monsieur Parrinì not being able to make his film, it must have seemed to her something like Michelangelo not being able to get hold of a block of marble, bless her heart.

"I'm in Milan," she said, leaving him stunned with surprise.

She wanted to talk to him. She was not alone. Did he have time for a dinner? They made a date for Sunday evening, at the Gallia restaurant, in Piazza Duca d'Aosta. Bissieu treated herself well, for a cowardly and fleeting moment Manlio Parrini hoped he wouldn't have to pay for the dinner.

The weekend had dragged on very slowly, boring. He had walked a bit, phoned his doctor friend who, however, was at a golf tournament and didn't have time to make conversation.

"Are you drinking? Smoking?" his friend asked him. He regretted calling him.

The only thrill came from the news on the Bastoni case, which was announced with various articles in the newspapers, even on the front page. Obviously, he chose to read the *Corriere*, in homage to his semi-friendship with Claudio Tarsi.

SENSATIONAL TURNABOUT
IN THE BASTONI MURDER: AN
INTERNATIONAL ARREST WARRANT

He read Tarsi's piece avidly, and then those of the other newspapers. Deputy Prosecutor Sensini has issued an international arrest warrant for Sophie Verraux, twenty-three years old, a Swiss citizen residing in Basel, romantically linked to Matteo D'Onofrio, the nephew of the victim found strangled on the morning of the . . . etc., etc. Since the young lady is lovely and the social media are full of her photographs, the newspapers wallow in it like never before, happy to throw a few bones to the hungry and morbid public. Sophie is beautiful, yes, blond, slender. She is a high-level model, someone who takes to the catwalk for Saint Laurent and Gucci, and manages, already at that age, her own brand of cosmetics, so the photos in the newspapers are of various types: the ones on the catwalks, and other more institutional ones, where she appears as a skincare entrepreneur, whatever that is, thinks Manlio Parrini.

The young lady must have a notable family behind her, of course, as demonstrated by the caliber of her lawyers. One, with more surnames than the king of Prussia, assures the press that it is an obvious misunderstanding, that he will not oppose any kind of request from the Milan prosecutor's office, that Miss Verraux is at the investigators' complete disposal. And also—Tarsi doesn't write this but makes it clear that the detail is not secondary—that they are expecting to receive the letters rogatory and the visit of the Italian magistrate who is dealing with the case.

Immediately, but probably not all that immediately.

Matteo D'Onofrio's lawyers, on the other hand, raise their heads a little. An arrest warrant, no less, for the girlfriend of their client confirms the ferocious overzealousness of the prosecutors, who, unable to solve the case, are shooting blindly hoping to intimidate a suspect. No one speaks of the Peruvian handyman, who is still in a cell in the Opera prison, and has no powerful lawyers.

Manlio Parrini drinks down the details, justifying himself with the fact that he has nothing to do, he is inactive, bored. He even thinks of calling Sensini, but obviously he lets that go. Claudio Tarsi, on the other hand, calls him.

"I was just reading your novels, Tarsi. The mystery of Villa Bastoni is getting more and more interesting."

"Ah, you've already read it, what a pity, I wanted to surprise you."

"Well, it's a real turning point, isn't it?" he says now, happy to be able to comment on the story with someone who knows a lot of things. "Sensini must certainly have some good cards in her hand this time, because in order to issue an international arrest warrant..."

"There is only one explanation, Parrini."

"And what's that?"

"A woman's blond hair on the corpse."

"Ah, yes, I forgot that."

"It seems that there were more people in that house on the morning of the murder than at the stadium."

"But you, Tarsi, excuse me... Can you see a rich and famous model, who is on the cover of *Vogue*, someone who frequents Place Vendôme the way you and I go to the pizzeria on the corner, strangling an old woman in Milan?"

Tarsi laughed, but not that much.

"Yes, you are right, Maestro, but who knows how people kill other people, what goes through their minds, what happens in those moments. And then... hasn't your De Angelis taught you anything? They kill the poor, Parrini, and they kill the rich, the educated, the ignorant..."

"Don't tell me that you started reading De Angelis!" This time he really laughed, a sincere laugh that combined surprise and admiration. That Tarsi was truly a phenomenon.

"Almost everything. Very pleasant, funny, terribly old-fashioned... Maybe that's what I like. Now I'm on *The Three Roses*,* woe to you if you tell me how it ends, even if in those detective stories every time a foreign name appears..."

They concluded the call with gruff and rough goodbyes, those "see yous" that could also mean that they would never see each other again, but the phone call had put Parrini in a good mood.

All that was left to do was get ready for dinner.

Standing in front of the closet he realizes that for an elegant evening, indeed something luxurious, no less

* Augusto De Angelis, *The Hotel of the Three Roses*.

than on the terrace of the Gallia, he is bereft. He has no decent clothes, that is, only two outfits, but he knows that when he puts them on he looks like a nouveau riche butcher at his daughter's wedding, so he gives up immediately. He had even bought a tailcoat once, or rather Anita had imposed it on him, for a ceremony at the Élysée, after *Broken Truths* won the prize at Cannes, and he had never worn it again. He laughs at the thought of showing up in a tailcoat in Piazza Duca d'Aosta . . . And why not in top hat and monocle?

Crazy old man.

In the end he dresses as usual, a good jacket and off he goes, because after all he is an artist, and he can do what he wants.

Nathalie Bissieu is as he remembered her, a beautiful abundant lady, bright, blond in an embarrassing way, with a noisy laugh, elegant enough not to make one suspect that it is an occasional elegance. The other diners are a gentleman in his fifties, in a suit and tie, the appearance of a very busy businessman who is taking a break, and a younger lady, in her thirties. Bissieu does the introductions: he is the lawyer Patrick Foscal, from Paris, and the lady is Catherine Lacroix, director of the Cinémathèque française. The pleasantries of high, indeed very high, society exhaust themselves with the aperitifs. They decide to speak in French. It seemed as if the man was the boss, but instead it is the young lady who carries the ball.

His interview with *Le Monde*, or rather, Bissieu's fine article, had kicked up the dust in the world of French cinephiles. Broadly speaking, there are those who think that the overwhelming power of American platforms is a godsend, but there are also those who argue that there must remain a space for auteur cinema, that at least something, at the highest levels of language and art, must be able to move freely. For some time now, the world of French cinema has been in turmoil, there is a desire for more Europe and fewer American superheroes, to put it simply, and many small producers, together with some institutions that boast large sponsors—she is talking about themselves—would welcome the return of Parrini under the banner of auteur cinema.

"More art and less market," Bissieu concluded, while the lawyer added his little wrinkle, arguing that the two things are not in open contradiction, that sometimes art, auteur cinema, works very well even at the box office, indeed in that case it is better, the niche does not interest us. He was the money man, of course.

Of course, the Maestro didn't have to say yes or no, it was just an evening in which they had the honor of meeting him, and telling him that he was not alone in his battle against the algorithm that writes the scripts and the marketing that designs the plots and chooses the casts.

In short, it was a matter of thinking about it, of pondering, of deciding whether such a battle—which he had to fight only by feeling totally free and making a good film—deserved to be fought. Otherwise, for them it would have been just a good dinner with friends, in Milan, *"cette ville si dynamique."*

The evening ended at the Gallia bar, just him and Bissieu. Now they could speak freely.

"They have the money," she says. "That's not a problem. They will pretend to put together a consortium of small producers, but they will do the bulk of it. We French take this cinema thing seriously, we don't like the Americans coming to march under the Eiffel Tower. And I would also add that the Ministry of Culture, in Paris, would consider it a nice coup to help produce Monsieur Parrinì's new masterpiece that no one in Italy wants to do."

He laughed:

"At the Ministry of Culture in Italy they probably don't even know who I am, I'm not a presenter of song contests or game shows," he said.

He was exaggerating, but not that much.

At half past eleven it was all over.

The proposal had been made, the cards were on the table. Manlio Parrini should have been over the moon, but instead he felt a little infusion of melancholy. He had rejected the emerging American star and other somewhat absurd conditions, and now he was about to accept the French grandeur, the chauvinism of the Sun King who was saying, "*Le cinéma c'est moi.*" Wasn't it, after all, the same thing? No, not the same thing, of course, but the same attitude, the same imperial logic.

He repeated to himself that he should really be happy, that he should tell the others that the film was no longer a hypothesis... Then he looked at his phone, four calls, in a crescendo of urgency, all from Sara De Viesti, who had then given up. "Where are you?" said the first. Then: "Fucking answer." Then again: "We're giving you half an hour." And the last one: "All right then, tomorrow morning at your place. Early."

Nothing else.

It's just past midnight. Manlio Parrini thinks of calling, but then drops it. Tomorrow morning, okay, present!

Now he wants to enjoy that moment of internal struggle between the Parrini happy for having found a producer and Parrini the nihilist who thinks that freedom does not exist, that it's always limited, always conditional. It will not be Luca Corrioni with the American producers and the Film Commission of Portofino, no. It will be the Arc de Triomphe and the French government that makes itself the champion of European culture. He is happy, of course, but deep down...

23

IT'S NOT EVEN EIGHT O'CLOCK, MANLIO PARRINI HAS just gotten up, waiting for the gurgling of the moka to become more intense, meanwhile he's enjoying the aroma and thinking about the night before. He should be jumping for joy, and instead he feels a strange anxiety clinging to him. What an idiot, he had blamed matters of principle, the sense of oppression of having a master, one who dictates the rules. Whether it was Luca Corrioni with his nonsense or the refined French millionaires on a mission for cultural grandeur, not much changed.

Now, however, he's looking at himself, in his underwear, in front of the bathroom mirror.

An old imbecile, it actually changes a lot.

And since that is the moment of sincerity, of total honesty with himself, of merciless examination, he must admit what he did not want to see last night, in a taxi, while reading Sara's messages. The anxiety, the dissatisfaction, the fear, do not stem from money or the producer of the film, but from the dread of not being able to do it. He had a technical alibi, until now, a nice shield behind which to say: it can't be done. And now he doesn't have it anymore, the story of the genius victim of conditioning and pressure doesn't hold up. Now it depends only on him, Manlio Parrini, Monsieur Parrinì, the Maestro... how had Bissieu put it? "The greatest filmmaker alive." She's a crazy old woman too! Well, now he was afraid of not being capable, of not being up to his great film of thirty years earlier. Having passed seventy, with his body failing, with the doctor telling him to buy a dog and play bocce, he had sucked energy from those enthusiastic young people, Sara, the lighting magician... a vampire feeding on young blood. But it was himself that he doubted, deep down, and...

The intercom.

Sara and the young historian burst into the house like a gust of wind.

"Would you like some coffee?"

"No, let's go!"

The car is Sara's, but Gianni is driving. They're gliding along, so to speak, out toward the lake, heedless, at first, of the questions that Parrini asks, a litany of where are we going and why, and make up your minds and tell me something. Then, when they are finally out of town, Sara opens up. They didn't know what to do, that Saturday and Sunday, so he—Gianni points out—had the idea of a tour around those parts, to make concentric circles around Bellagio and go and see the surroundings...but not the surroundings... the cemeteries.

They are sad and beautiful places, small village cemeteries, or of towns just a little bigger than a neighborhood of Milan. They searched a little, talked a little, looked around a little. The lake, and the areas of the lake, have this strange air of suspension between the city that colonized them and a grumpy peace that closes them like a hedgehog.

They started from Bellagio, of course, and then circled around, like eagles hunting: the cemetery of Canzo, the tiny cemetery of Ballabio. The monumental cemetery of Lecco would be left for last, because it is big, and because they had decided that it would be the last attempt, the end of the route. Small mountain graveyards, some overlooking the lake, in panoramic points where you would expect to see the villa of some wealthy Milanese, but no, death still counts for something, fortunately, or it did once, because they are all ancient cemeteries, some with a register of burials and others with nothing, not even the guardian's hut, just small paths of pebbles between the tombs, a wall for ossuaries, a tap for those who want to change the water for flowers.

And then they found it. When they had almost given up—not that they had believed in it much from the beginning... In short, yes, it had been a stroke of luck, but also the prize for their desperate attempt, bordering on idiocy.

Now all three are in the cemetery of Maggianico, which is now the outskirts of Lecco, a small cemetery at the foot of the hill, behind the church of Sant'Andrea. Standing erect, almost at attention, in front of a simple white tombstone:

STEFANO ASTARITA
(2-4-1880 – 19-8-1949)

The small black-and-white photo, in an oval frame, shows a handsome, vigorous man, taken half-length in his Carabinieri's uniform. The plaque next to it, the same, identical, reads:

ANDREINA CASPIANI ASTARITA
(13-1-1889 – 23-11-1957)

His wife. She also has her photograph, but it was taken when the lady was already a certain age, you can't tell if she was a beautiful woman, even if Manlio Parrini thinks that someone born in those years, who had seen two world wars, had to be a beautiful woman perforce, kind of a silly idea.

Sara and the young, lovestruck historian, hopelessly so, that much is sure, spoke with the priest, a new, Black priest, originally from Togo, only recently ordained, who knew nothing about the cemetery, but directed them to an old local man who was doing work for the parish. He sent them to another local, a withered old woman. They went to talk to her.

Yes, the Astaritas still lived in the area, someone went, not every year but most, on November 2, All Souls' Day, to lay flowers on the tomb of the old carabiniere and his wife, but she didn't know who or where to find them. There was an Astarita who had a mechanic's workshop, just outside the village, but had closed a while ago. Then the old woman became suspicious, perhaps because these are questions you don't get asked every day, ones about a grave in the cemetery, or perhaps because Sara De Viesti's bushy red hair can alarm any female creature on the planet.

Manlio Parrini listens incredulously to the story, but he can't take his eyes off the small photo of the major of the Royal Carabinieri Stefano Astarita, who died at the age of sixty-nine, the man who had captured the murderer of Augusto De Angelis. The look he exchanges with Sara says it all, and she understands immediately. This one, this gentleman who wanted the photo in uniform on the grave, must come into the story, must have a part in their film. Sara smiles because she has understood. The young historian no, he hasn't understood anything, he may be so lost that he thinks Sara is smiling at him.

Anyway, they abandoned the search at dinnertime. Sara sent him some messages later that night, but he didn't respond.

Now they're on the state road that leads to Calolziocorte, along the lake, to the south, the Lecco branch of Lake Como. Probably Manzoni's ghost is hovering all around them, but they don't see it. The workshop the old woman spoke of, if that's the right one, is on the ground floor of a red building, a little peeling, which could use a little work on the facade. The two shutters are closed, the place looks abandoned. On the intercoms there are two names, they ring one at random. Nothing. They ring the other one. Instead of answering the intercom, a lady looks out of a window on the second floor. They ask her about the mechanic. "It's been closed for a year," she says, shouting from the window.

"And do you know where..."

"Wait, I'll come down."

Perhaps the lady does not want to miss an opportunity to gossip, to tell her friends, she thought they were looking for a mechanic, instead it seems that they are looking for the one who used to work there, their car is not broken down. Once she gets down, she stays standing in the half-open door. Astarita has been closed for a few years, she does not know if the workshop is up for sale or if they're going to rent it out, for now it's empty. She hopes they won't make a Chinese restaurant out of it, "because of the stench that would come up toward the windows," she says.

Astarita has retired, no, she doesn't really know where he lives, but in the area, she believes, maybe in Lecco... That is, if he is still alive.

"But..." The lady has remembered something and now she doesn't know whether to say it. "Why are you looking for him?"

Manlio Parrini had an answer prepared.

"Oh, he's an old friend I've lost track of. We happened to be passing by the lake and I thought I would say hello to him..."

A little weak, but the lady falls for it, her suspicions must not have been so strong, after all.

"I know that the daughter is a pharmacist nearby, in Olginate, her name is Katia."

They go beyond the lake, not even two miles, and look for the pharmacy in Olginate. Only Parrini and Sara De Viesti go in, they wait until a customer has finished with their prescriptions and then turn to the pharmacist behind the counter.

"Dr. Katia? Katia Astarita?"

She looks at them a little suspiciously, but even more with curiosity. She is a woman over fifty, with a white coat.

"Yes, it's me . . . sorry, no one calls me Astarita, that's my maiden name . . . everyone calls me Carraghi here, my husband's name . . ."

Gentle, but her voice has a clear interrogative tone. What she's really saying is: "Who are you? What do you want?"

They explain themselves in some way, interrupting if a customer enters, and then resuming the conversation. They are doing a little historical research and have come across the figure of . . . her great-grandfather, right? Major Stefano Astarita, who was a carabiniere in Bellagio . . .

Now more than confounded, the woman is dumbfounded. Her great-grandfather? She knows nothing about him, for sure. Maybe her father . . . But what research? About what?

Sara De Viesti explains to her that they are collecting material for a documentary on the Carabinieri, that they are looking for news on the dissolution of the corps, in 1944, which . . . A customer enters, the woman has somehow understood that it is nothing personal, nothing serious. As soon as she has counted out change, she picks up the phone and starts a call, speed-dialed.

"Dad . . ."

When she ends the call, she strongly advises them: "He is still with it, but don't tire him out, he is almost ninety years old."

Antonio Astarita is waiting for them at the door of a house just outside Carenno. They had to cross back over to the branch of the lake that turns to the south, climb a little, go around a few curves.

He is a very old gentleman, quite fit, however, lucid, amazed like his daughter, perhaps more so. He invites them in, but Manlio Parrini says that they don't want to disturb him, on the contrary, it's lunchtime, why don't they look for a trattoria and make themselves comfortable? He seems happy with that break from his routine, closes the house, and after not even ten minutes they are sitting under a pergola overlooking the lake, from above, with a bottle of red wine and a plate of local cold cuts and cheeses in front of them. To start with, that's great.

Manlio Parrini tells the story, in broad strokes, explains why they are curious, why they want to know about his grandfather. Sara De Viesti was thinking of taking out her notebook but she changed her mind immediately, she does not want to give the impression of recording, probably that would make him become more circumspect, more prudent.

In short, he has good memories of his grandfather, because as a child he spent summers with him and his grandmother, in the house in Carenno, he lived with his father and mother, of course, in Lecco, but he spent the summers with his grandparents. He remembers well the stories that his grandfather told him about the war, about the Carabinieri. He knew that at a certain point he had to flee, that he had managed to go to Switzerland with his grandmother, then they had returned after the war. He had died in 1949, when the grandson was eleven years old... he is buried in the cemetery of Maggianico, every once in a while he goes to visit him, but not often... His father was a mechanic, in Lecco, during the war he had been a prisoner and had learned that trade from the Americans, near Cassino, and the grandson too had opened a workshop, on the state road, nearby, and had stayed there for forty years. Then he had said enough—"I don't understand anything about today's cars anymore, some don't even have engines"—and he had retired to his grandparents' house, because selling it was not convenient, he had a nice garden, it was fine. He had left his father's house, in Lecco, to his daughter, who had gone to the university and was a pharmacist, "But you know that..."

Going to talk about his carabiniere grandfather to an over eighty-year-old who has retired to a kind of hermitage, far away from everything, produces a certain effect. Antonio Astarita certainly did not expect to have to exhume memories of when he was eight, ten years old, it is something that explodes in his hands, all that past, the excursions in the woods, his knees always scraped. His grandfather taught him tricks and games, how to recognize the edible mushrooms... Then he remembers that he had fallen ill, and had died. His grandmother had been left alone in the house in Carenno, and he had begun to spend his summers elsewhere... He is battling with nostalgia, he does not hide it.

"What I have left from my grandfather, I found it at home when my grandmother also died, is a carabiniere's uniform, and a hat, plus a few photographs, their wedding picture... Then there are some letters, I think, that he wrote to her when she was already in Switzerland and he hadn't gone yet... but who knows where they might be."

The young historian Gianni had a flash in his eye. The letters of a carabiniere to his wife, in 1943, in 1944... for someone who is doing a doctorate in Contemporary History, who has done his thesis on diaries... wow!

"And can we see these letters?"

"Ah, I'd have to look for them... but let's try."

He went to take a nap, he was tired, he had eaten too much—he said this in a tone of grateful reproach. First, he had taken them to the cellar, two damp and dark rooms that were accessed via a fairly uneven wooden ladder. The light came in through two skylights that were opaque with dirt, he had shown them a light switch before retiring, but the bulb gave out such a dim light that it was almost useless.

"If there is something, it is here, look for it . . . There is nothing to steal," he added. "Give a shout when you've finished, I'll make you coffee."

Now they're looking at each other. The situation is absurd: Manlio Parrini, Sara De Viesti, and a young historian, in the midst of crates and boxes, an old cupboard full of tools, a few sealed bags, soft, perhaps blankets or old clothes. It's a place no one has come down to for years, the dust says that, the cobwebs say it, even the fingerprints on the shelves are ancient.

After half an hour, they find a bunch of envelopes, at the bottom of a box a little moist from humidity. Twenty-one envelopes, tied with a black shoelace, all, except three, addressed to Andreina Caspiani Astarita, at Famiglia Varesi, via Baroffio 32, Locarno, CH. The stamps are orange, with the fasces and the inscription "Repubblica Sociale Italiana," 2.50 lire. They contain only one sheet, at most two, written in pen, dense, with a pointy but precise handwriting, Sara has to turn on the flashlight on her phone to illuminate them well.

They all begin with the date and "Andreina dearest." The first was in January 1944, Major Astarita is reassuring his wife, who had gone to work with a family in Switzerland. There is some mention of his son, wounded, seriously, and hospitalized near Rome. The major blesses the Lord, because the boy is safe, in an area now firmly controlled by the Americans, at least for him the war is over. He writes in very brief notes about the situation in Bellagio, now there are only three of them, at the Carabinieri station, squeezed between the German command that barely tolerates them and the Fascist militia that considers them possible traitors. They do small checks, stuff related to rationing cards and the black market, thefts of animals and crops from local farmers, things the Germans do not deal with.

In a letter dated March 1944—Major Astarita never puts the date in Roman numerals for the year of the Fascist era—he speaks of "a very bad atmosphere" and of the rumors that are circulating, that the Carabinieri will soon be disbanded. "What else can I do, Andreina dear, I'll stay at my post, as long as I can."

In another letter, April 28, 1944, he tells more about his son, who managed to send him a message through a merchant in Lecco who had crossed the lines, returning home from Rome. He is fine, officially he's a prisoner, but since he is good with engines he has made an agreement with the doctors at the American hospital, and they do not discharge him, he is listed as convalescent, and in the meantime he repairs some vehicles. "Our Angelo is learning English!" jokes the major. He adds that he has already given the good news to his daughter-in-law and grandson, who are evacuees near Varese. In the letters there is never an expression of affection, a declaration of love, not even an "I miss you"—he had to be a carabiniere even in his human relationships, rigid and concise—the letters read like reports, only in one, at the end, there is an "I think of you."

Then they find what in some way, without realizing it, they are looking for. It is a letter dated July 6, 1944, it begins with the usual formal greetings, but then tells of an episode of a few days earlier.

> *Three scoundrels massacred a gentleman, here in Bellagio, with such rough violence as to leave him half dead. A writer, I learned later, suspected of anti-fascism, moreover, and they, the aggressors, three Fascists evacuated from Milan. We detained one of them, thanks to the athletic ability of our colleague Casiraghi, lucky him who is young, he threw himself into the fray with a fury, and the other two fled. For the report to be provided to the German command and the militia, I had to invent a stupid story of passion, perhaps of cheating, adding a made-up female figure who supposedly made them fight out of jealousy, generating a fight and then vanishing. I hope they believe it, that they don't do any further investigation, that they settle for this hasty report that is not important to them. But what can you do, Andreina, leaving out the political violence was the only way to keep the culprit in jail, because if I had mentioned a purge they would have released him immediately. If they interro-*

gate him, I'll be in some real hot water, but they have other things to do these days. You see how things are, Andreina, a carabiniere forced to lie, to declare a falsehood in a report, it's not right... But these are the times we're in. It's only a question of time, by now, very little time, until everything collapses...

Manlio Parrini looked Sara De Viesti straight in the eyes, for a long time, with an intensity that surprised both of them. Neither of them said a word, but there were many things in that look, there was the last piece of the puzzle that fell into place, there was the film's final scene, there was also, perhaps, who knows, a bit of justice for Augusto De Angelis. Not true justice, which would never come again, which already had been sealed with signatures and stamps, its lawyerly and procedural blessings, but the justice of a recomposed truth.

Major Astarita's last letter was from a few days later, a few lines.

Bellagio, 17 July 1944

Andreina dearest,
the decision is made, tomorrow night, when there is no moon, I will try to cross the border by certain paths that I know, it will be a long walk, may God make it a good one. I asked the young Casiraghi if he wants to join

the adventure, but he wouldn't give me a straight answer. I suspect he wants to join the partisan bands, the other day he told me that there are also monarchists up there in the mountains, I hope all the best for him. If everything goes well, then, in three or four days I will be able to hug you again. Don't be anxious, what God wants will happen.
Farewell from your husband,
Stefano

The return journey was quiet, they were all very tired. Young Gianni drove, there was not much traffic because they were going in the opposite direction to the flow of those returning to Brianza from Milan, after working all day. A sunset blurred by a light mist colored the last hills before the great flat plain.

"In the end it was a cold case," said Manlio Parrini.

"That's right," replied Sara De Viesti.

"There was no woman," he concluded.

Then he invited them to dinner—"But no Chinese or Indian, eh!" he said—and sent some messages to their other colleagues. If they were tired, or didn't want to spend a few more hours with him, they didn't say so.

At nine they were in the annex, at nine ten their food was delivered from a nearby trattoria where they were used to Parrini's calls. Then the wizard of lights, Scotti, and Marras also arrived for coffee and liqueurs.

And then Manlio Parrini went into the kitchen and returned with a bottle of champagne.

To celebrate the closure of the case, the letters to the wife of Major Astarita, to toast the story that was coming to an end, Sara De Viesti was thinking.

But no. Manlio Parrini says that a decision must be made, and that it must be made by everyone, because they are a collective, so he proposes to vote.

"We have a producer," he says.

The gaze of those others becomes very attentive, more than attentive, four pairs of eyes that do not want to look at anything else.

"A consortium of independent French producers, coordinated by the Cinémathèque."

"Conditions?" asks Sara De Viesti.

"None," says Monsieur Parrinì. He explains that the consortium seems a bit like a cover, that the real money will be put in by a more traditional structure, but in short...

"They'll lay the red carpet under the Arc de Triomphe... a sacrifice we can bear, I would say."

Now they drink, laugh, talk over each other, ask for details, get excited, ask still more questions. The De Angelis collective is shining bright.

I feel so alive, thinks Manlio Parrini.

24

IT HADN'T ALL BEEN SO DARK, THOUGH. NOT ALWAYS.

He realizes that he is no longer posing resistance, that hanging on is useless. Of course, it didn't have to be this way. That end, more than killing him, offends him. Dying from the beating of some thugs, in the street, was certainly not what he had imagined. And to die now, moreover, what a mockery. Many times he had imagined the "after" after the war, after the disaster into which that scoundrel on the balcony of Piazza Venezia had dragged them all. To be able to go back to writing, without oversight this time, without the fear of having a manuscript sent back to you with notes of the corrections to be made... less turbid settings! Less psychological lucubrations! Maybe being able to write some all-Italian plot, with Italian characters, with an Italian murderer... Ah, what nonsense.

Or even returning to the theater, which was his love. Breathing once again that feverish and suspended air that is behind the curtain before the house lights go out, dealing with actors, actresses, critics...That was not the world he was seeing now, that he had seen for the past decade.

Who knows if after, after all that, and after his death, someone would still read the adventures of Inspector De Vincenzi, if some publisher, once the censorship and prohibitions had fallen, would start to republish his detective stories. He didn't dare hope for that, but...And who knows if one day, as in America, as in England, as in France, it would be possible to write about suspense and mystery, about murder victims, about inspectors who intuit the culprit not from evidence, but from psychological investigation, without being considered mere entertainers, authors of streetcar books. Who knows, maybe someone, then, will remember that he, Augusto De Angelis, had said it.

> Certainly, sir, even the persecutor of a murderer can be a poet, when he bends over the ground trodden by a sole and a heel, when he examines the ashes of a cigarette, when he deduces from a lost strand of hair the presence of the murderer. It is his brain that flies, at that moment [. . .]

No, really, sir, I have no remorse about writing detective novels today.

This too is a way of making verses.*

It's a bad time, the one in which you are forced to think about what will remain of you after. If indeed anything will remain.

What weariness, though. What lethargy.

What cruelty, to take every breath fearing that it is your last.

* Augusto De Angelis, "Lecture on the Detective Story."

25

THINGS PRECIPITATED. WHILE THEY WERE BUSY WAN-dering around cemeteries and mountain villages perched above the lake, damp cellars full of memories of the past, and improvised parties, the Bastoni case marked another sensational turning point.

Manlio Parrini was hardly thinking about it anymore, in fact he wasn't thinking about it at all. He had spent the night in a pleasant catatonic state, half conscious and half not. He looked at the alarm clock, 2:28, and thought about the things to do, which were millions, the cast, the auditions...A minute passed and the alarm clock struck ten past five, and he was thinking about the sound engineer, the work on the sounds...Then it was half past seven and he was thinking of Sara De Viesti: they would have to rewrite the last scenes, put Major Astarita in them. He remembers that reading his letters to his wife—“Andreina dearest”—he had felt almost physically that drop in light that they had planned, that fading, that graying toward darkness, the disaster, the end of everything.

Then he would have to call Bissieu and say that he accepted the French proposal, which the collective had voted unanimously, but on one condition: she would have to act as a liaison between money and art, between producers and the set. Yes, maybe that wasn’t her job, but why not? She had started the thing and he was dragging her into the history of cinema, an exchange that she would accept.

Now that he has finally gotten up, and is mentally lining up the priorities of the day—but perhaps he should say of the weeks, of the months to come—he catches himself avidly reading the newspaper. Not the usual distracted browsing, but two dense pages, to drink down line by line. The main headline has a very evident capsule on the front page:

TWO CULPRITS FOR ONE CRIME?
THE PROSECUTOR’S TRUTH ABOUT THE
BASTONI MURDER

Press conference of Deputy Prosecutor Chiara
Sensini after her trip to Switzerland—The
international warrant for Sophie Verraux has been

withdrawn—Upcoming indictment for Matteo D'Onofrio and Carlos Manolo Pinzago

Manlio Parrini made himself comfortable.

Claudio Tarsi had unleashed his qualities as a storyteller, because he had space available, finally, and because in addition to the new details, of which there were many, he had to retrace the whole story.

He starts with an account of Sensini's trip to Switzerland. There had probably been contact between the prosecutors, and perhaps even some phone calls at a higher level, political, or diplomatic, to speed up the process and clarify what to all intents and purposes seemed to be a mistake. Miss Verraux's lawyers had given their full and immediate availability to meet with the Italian investigators, even bypassing the judicial bureaucracy and some rules, and Sensini had rushed to Basel accompanied by two bigwigs of the judicial police and the recommendations of the chief prosecutor, who feared an international incident.

During the meeting in Basel, which was also attended by the girl, irrefutable evidence had been presented in defense of the suspect, the object no less of an arrest warrant. On the morning of the murder, September 6, Sophie Verraux had presented her new collection of self-tanning creams, made in co-production and co-marketing with Chanel, no less. She had spent the first hours of the day in makeup, then a driver had taken her from Basel to

Geneva, where dozens of journalists and influencers from the beauty industry had attended the event, culminating in a gala lunch, followed by individual interviews with various newspapers and a grueling photo shoot. The whole thing had lasted until six in the evening, without a moment's respite for the young Verraux. For Chiara Sensini, nothing the lawyers said was new: she followed social media, too, she too had done some research, of course, and she knew that the girl's Instagram profile was full of photographs of the event of that day.

And the warrant, then?

Simple: the girl had to explain how two blond hairs, hers, had ended up on the corpse of an old lady in Milan, who was incidentally her boyfriend's great-aunt. The warrant was partly an obligatory measure and partly an instrument for pressuring other suspects, that is, her Italian boyfriend.

Manlio Parrini smiles, alone in his living room, still messy from the revelry of the De Angelis collective the night before. Tarsi keeps in reserve some twists and turns to keep the reader's attention. He pretends he is writing a chronicle but in reality he is designing a plot, he goes back and forth on the timescale to amaze the reader. And he succeeds. Parrini thinks that maybe introducing him to good detective stories, even if from the thirties, helped him write such a dense piece.

But how did Sensini know, without analysis, without DNA samples, without evidence, that the hair on the old woman's body was Verraux's?

That is the real ace up the sleeve of the prosecutor's office, and judging by the story of the *Corriere*, Sensini extracts it with a certain satisfaction, as if she were responding to all those who had criticized her, who pressured her, who wanted to take the investigation away from her, even send an inspector from the Ministry.

In D'Onofrio's car, the one with the double bottom in the back seat, they had found some material, initially considered uninteresting. The things you find in cars, more or less: sunglasses, telephone cables, a few scattered receipts and ads, the green envelope of a parking fine, not even opened, and a small beauty bag containing lipstick, a small mirror with powder, two tubes of mascara, and a brush. On the brush, a few blond hairs, which Forensics had compared with the two strands found on the corpse of Nora Vuillermoz, the widow Bastoni. It was the same hair, without a doubt.

How did the hairs end up there?

Sensini had left Basel and said goodbye cordially to the girl's lawyers, who were pleased and determined to give the highest prominence to the news that their client, the owner of the world-famous Verraux Peau Douce brand, had nothing to do with that ugly story. Probably the girl's social media managers were already studying how to make an advertising campaign out of it. Sensini, after a phone call with the chief prosecutor in Milan, had issued a statement in which she thanked the Swiss authorities and the girl's lawyers for having contributed to a rapid resolution of such a thorny case and helped justice, the arrest warrant was dropped, of course, after the "complete and exhaustive" clarifications.

All that remained was to summon the young D'Onofrio, which Sensini had done urgently right on Sunday morning, and after an interrogation that Tarsi defines as "dramatic" the boy had given yet another of his versions.

Yes, it is true, he had arrived at the villa on the morning of September 6. He had also gone there the night before, to pick up a package, but his old aunt had told him to come back the next day, because the package was not complete.

Now that he has to dodge a charge of voluntary homicide—from thirty years to life imprisonment—the young D'Onofrio is willing to admit many things, even that he was his aunt's mule that carried boxes of cash to Switzerland. His lawyers are trying to limit the damage, they say they are ready to provide the coordinates of the accounts, in Lugano, Bern, and Basel, into which, for at least three years, their client has deposited, every three or four months, the proceeds of the illegal activities of the widow Bastoni, i.e., the cash from the rents paid under the table.

But the most absurd revelation the young D'Onofrio makes almost immediately, when he realizes that he cannot deny it. According to his story, a little disjointed and confused, he had arrived at the villa around half past eleven, had found his aunt dead, lying on the carpet, with her legs under the desk, he was upset and had run away immediately. Getting into the car, however, trembling and beside himself, he had thought that perhaps his aunt had marked down the appointment of that morning somewhere, or left some trace that could lead to him, place him at the scene of the crime, and with the things that would come out, the business, the rents, the money, his position would be very difficult. Then he had thought about trying to mislead the investigation, but how? He had to hurry. Then he had seen, in the glove compartment, his girlfriend's little cosmetics case, which she kept in the car for convenience. He had taken some hair from the brush, had run back to the villa and deposited it on the corpse. Something, he had thought, that would rattle the brains of the investigators, that would maybe have left the case an unresolved mystery.

And here Claudio Tarsi, the good reporter, puts his own spin on it: it would have been enough to throw away that beauty case, make the brush disappear, eliminate that trace, and really the investigators would have gone crazy trying to trace that hair, which in fact they had been doing for weeks. Instead, he had put the beauty case back in the glove compartment. One word is missing, "idiot," which Tarsi does not say, of course, but the whole story seems constructed for the reader to say so.

The interrogation ended in the worst way: a request for indictment for voluntary homicide, combined with a request for the revocation of house arrest.

And Pinzago?

Claudio Tarsi opens a new chapter of the story. Carlos Manolo Pinzago is detained in the Opera prison, also on charges of voluntary homicide. For now, he refuses to answer the investigators' questions, but it may be that the new developments will convince him to change his mind.

The ending of Tarsi's article—Parrini read it with such attention that he let his coffee go cold—is amazing.

> As in a detective story of yesteryear, there are two alleged murderers for a single corpse. What would the old inspectors of the past have done, we wonder—the protagonists of detective novels without cameras and without cell phones. An American-style confrontation, perhaps, or perhaps one of those sessions of reflection and analysis, in the presence of the two

defendants, hoping that one of the two would betray himself, or using one to "frame" the other. At the moment, despite the success of the investigations conducted with a cunning worthy of a Maigret by Deputy Prosecutor Sensini, even at the cost of friction with the head of the prosecutor's office, it is still not known who really killed the widow Bastoni. And as in an old detective novel, we are waiting for the final pages of the story.

Manlio Parrini made himself another cup of coffee, poured the cold and undrinkable one in the sink.

While waiting for the moka to do its duty, he picks up the phone. Claudio Tarsi answers immediately, perhaps he was expecting the call.

"Bravo, Tarsi, excellent article, it kept me in suspense."

"It's that you never account for chance, Maestro, and the chance that someone can be so stupid as to put his girlfriend's hair on a corpse, and keep other strands of it in his car, is really imponderable. Not even your De Angelis would have thought of it."

"Ah, that's for sure. But I saw that you quote Maigret, at the end of your piece . . . Why not Commissioner De Vincenzi, then?"

"Because everyone knows Maigret, Parrini, while De Vincenzi no, until someone makes a film about him, of course."

"And what do you know about that, Tarsi?"

"Knowing things is my job, Parrini. Or should I call you Monsieur Parrinì? Remember that we have a deal."

Now he doesn't know whether to get irritated or laugh, but deep down he doesn't care, and even the other seems to give no weight to those skirmishes between men, who make fun of each other and prick each other like teenagers.

"In any case, there was no woman," says Tarsi.

He means no woman at the scene of the Bastoni murder, but Manlio Parrini immediately thinks of something else. There was no woman, no, not even at the scene of the De Angelis murder, and this brings him back to the things that really matter, the film, the work to be done, the anxiety that seizes him every time he feels called to that test.

He says goodbye quickly and goes back to the 1930s.

26

BETWEEN ECHOES OF THE CRIME NEWS AND SMALL news reports of the day, there is not much to choose from in the *Corriere della Sera* of Thursday, July 27, 1944.

At the trotting races at San Siro, the Bellagio prize (60,000 lire, 1,600 meters), Napoleon won, "vigorously opposed in the final by Mercede."

But there is also other news, some good, some bad.

PICKPOCKET TAKES TWO WATCHES

The merchant Giuseppe Conti, son of Pietro, from Gavirate, riding tram line 15 yesterday morning was adroitly pickpocketed. Conti kept two watches in the pockets of his vest—one gold, the other silver—tied together by a gold chain: the thief, after cutting the buttonhole of Conti's vest, slipped the two watches out of the pockets, without being noticed.

By the time the shopkeeper found out that he had been robbed, it was too late.

What times, eh! Of course, taking the tram with two precious watches...

> FEDERAL COMMISSIONER VISITS REFUGEE FAMILIES Yesterday afternoon, the Fascist federal commissioner visited a school where many refugee families from Rome, Florence, and Apuania have found shelter. He brought everyone some clothing and a pair of shoes for each. Costa was then given more detailed information about the various families and arranged to provide help for their most urgent needs.

And then, at the bottom of the page, small, without even a title:

> OBITUARY. The journalist and writer Augusto De Angelis has died. He made his debut in journalism at the age of 16 at *Vita*: he was then at the Stefani Agency, at the *Resto del Carlino*, at the *Ambrosiano*, at the *Sera*. He wrote eleven plays. Notable is his activity as a writer of detective stories.*

A rather tardy obituary. Augusto De Angelis had died ten days earlier, on July 18, 1944.

---

* *Corriere della Sera*, July 27, 1944.

27

CARLOS MANOLO PINZAGO COMMITTED SUICIDE IN HIS cell in the Opera prison. The prison officers found him early in the morning, hanged with a sheet tied to the bars of the window. Pinzago was in solitary confinement and, theoretically, under strict surveillance. He was fifty-two years old, with a wife, Maria, and a son. It is the eighty-second case of suicide in Italian prisons since the beginning of the year, a shameful record, worthy of an uncivilized country.

As far as is known, Pinzago did not leave messages, let alone confessions about the murder of the widow Bastoni, he killed himself and that's it. The prosecutor's office has opened an investigation that will go nowhere, it will die as he did. Indeed, with less fuss.

Manlio Parrini read the news and just about froze, an empty hole opened up in his gut, what happens when you take a sudden fall, or witness an injustice that is too unjust, that your senses don't have time to cushion. Despite the hectic days, the thousand things to do, the sheets full of notes with the scenes to be shot during the third day on the set of his new film, he sat motionless on a kitchen stool, his coffee in front of him, his eyes staring into space.

He had followed the case of the widow Bastoni from the beginning, from the first minutes. He had somehow taken part in it, as an extra, but also as an actor, he had done some favors for Deputy Prosecutor Chiara Sensini, had almost made friends with the reporter Claudio Tarsi, had read the news reports without skipping a single episode, as if it were a nineteenth-century installment novel, or one of those serial mysteries that Augusto De Angelis published in the newspapers. The mystery of Villa Bastoni—the villa a few yards from his windows—had been a small pastime for him, a riddle, a brainteaser with twists and turns to follow. And even for the widow Bastoni, who was also his neighbor, whom he had greeted many times, or met in the courtyard, he had not felt much empathy: she was the victim in a murder case, of course, a minimum of fellow feeling was part of the package. But as in Conan Doyle's novels, with Sherlock Holmes and Watson sniffing around and distinguishing between cigarette and pipe ashes, drawing who knows what certainties, his pain had never shown, his pity for the poor strangled old woman had crouched in the background, without ever being seen.

Now, however, the handyman Carlos had died, and died in that way.

He had sat on his sofa, he recalls, a few days after the murder, wondering what would become of him, asking if there might be a job for him. An Indigenous cube with the face of someone who had just come out of the forest, but who washed the Mercedes of the "mistress" with care, went shopping and brought back the exact change. Could he have been the murderer? Probably. He had had the means, the opportunity, and perhaps even the motive, he had tampered with the evidence at the crime scene, he had lied. In ten years of service with the widow Bastoni he must have come to know something about the woman's shady affairs, perhaps he was blackmailing her, perhaps there had been an argument on the morning of September 6, more than an argument, with him putting his hands around her neck... Yes, it was the most likely scenario, also the easiest and most obvious. His arrest had not raised protests or complaints, the newspapers had not spent half a word on his behalf.

But all this changes nothing. Manlio Parrini stares into space for a few minutes, thinks about what must go through the head of a man who removes the sheet from the bed, rolls it up to create a kind of rope, tests its resistance, and knots it to the bars. Think of how his heart must beat, how he must gasp for breath, what indecent determination must command the obedience of such a ferocious gesture against oneself.

He realizes that now, with the death of one of the two defendants in the murder of the widow Bastoni, the case is no longer a matter of a mystery novel, no longer theoretical. It is flesh and blood, violence, death. It becomes something irremediable and suspended forever, without justice, without forgiveness or remission.

It is another broken truth, thinks Maestro Parrini. Broken like the life of that kind Indigenous man who perhaps was also a murderer. An irremediable truth, like the one that will be the truth about the Bastoni crime, to which it will be difficult to give an answer, because of the two alleged culprits one is no longer there, he will not be able to defend himself or shout his innocence.

And the real problem, the problem of all times and everyone, Manlio Parrini now thinks, is not that truths are broken, but that there are no truths, that they simply do not exist. They are made of an ambiguous and mushy substance, diaphanous. The truths we know are only those that we admit as such, that we decide are truths. They have our stamp, our approval.

Augusto De Angelis was another truth without truth. A woman who had denounced him had been a limited-time truth, a useful truth, which had broken in a cellar on the hills of Lake Como, under the murky light of a bulb less luminous than Sara De Viesti's red hair. And other truths had been constructed about him and his life, a rock climb clinging to the hand- and footholds of what he had left: the books, the stories, the reflections. Nothing was true, nothing. Yet some truth was necessary, perforce.

Now there was that truth of a dead man in a cell, and it was an irrefutable truth, cold, stiff, impossible to deny, which nevertheless took with it who knows which and how many other truths: who had put his hands around the neck of the widow Bastoni? Who had squeezed until she was breathless forever?

The doorbell rang discreetly, respectfully. The driver from the production company had arrived to take him to the set, they were shooting the interiors, for now, today they had four scenes, quite complicated, a lot of work. Saverio Protti had turned out to be an excellent De Angelis, while Ardenzi, surprisingly, was a perfect De Vincenzi.

When he made himself comfortable in the car seat, in the back, like a real boss with his driver, his phone rang. He looked at the display: Claudio Tarsi. Yes, he was expecting it.

"So the case is closed, Maestro," he said without even saying hello.

"You think so, Tarsi? And the other defendant? The fool nephew?"

"The dead are always wrong, Maestro, especially if the living have good lawyers. A nice plea bargain for exporting capital, a crime punished less than the theft of a snack from a supermarket, plus evidence tampering, perhaps obstruction of justice, things like that. I could bet on two or three years with a suspended sentence, what do you say, do you want to bet?"

"Your cynicism is revolting, Tarsi."

"Yes, I've been told that before, but in my profession, that's considered a virtue."

The set was in a beautiful house in Porta Romana, rented for the occasion from the owner, who had had to move for two weeks, and Marras had refurnished everything, finding precious pieces who knows where, period furniture. They had to change the chandeliers, repaint, transform a modern apartment into an upper-middle-class house from the 1930s.

There is already a fair amount of confusion, it seems that everyone is moving around frantically and aimlessly, but actually everyone knows what they're doing. Ferdinando Scotti is giving crisp orders to his technicians, where to put the lights, which filters to prepare. Sara De Viesti, with the script in hand, is talking to the actors: Cosimo Ardenzi, who plays Commissioner De Vincenzi, a woman dressed as a maid, complete with a white apron over a black dress, and an elegant old lady, who is listening without saying anything.

"Everything all right?" asks Manlio Parrini, it's a kind of greeting.

"We are ready to shoot," says Sara De Viesti.

A lady in her forties, a folder in hand, writes something on a sheet of paper and calls everyone. Now there is a movement that seems synchronized, everyone goes to their places, the sound engineers put on their headphones, the actors place themselves in their assigned positions, Manlio Parrini and Sara De Viesti sit in front of two monitors side by side, Ferdinando Scotti does the same behind some other screens. The elderly actress, not without effort, lies down on a carpet, a makeup artist approaches to give her the last touches of powder, to dry some shiny lines she has on her face.

The lady in her forties also puts the clapperboard in front of a camera:

"De Angelis, four nine."

Manlio Parrini says:

"Quiet... Camera... Action!"

Zoom in on the young maid, she is twisting her apron in her hands, her face is upset and streaked with tears. A uniformed officer approaches the front door, opens it. Commissioner Carlo De Vincenzi enters with a light, almost hesitant step, followed by agent Cruni, a big man with a good-natured face, who is now tense and frowning.

UNIFORMED POLICEMAN: Here we are, inspector... As you ordered, nothing has been touched.

The inspector does not even look at the old woman's corpse lying on the ground, but walks with small steps throughout the room, looking out through the internal doors, one opening onto another living room, one onto a corridor. He turns to the maid, who is still wringing her apron.

INSPECTOR DE VINCENZI: And you, have you touched anything?
MAID: Nothing, Inspector...yes, I shook the lady...I brought smelling salts, but... she was cold... cold!
She bursts into tears.

Agent Cruni has disappeared into the other rooms, for a quick search.

Only now does Inspector De Vincenzi bend over the corpse of the old woman on the ground, place one knee on the carpet, and observe closely.

INSPECTOR DE VINCENZI (TO THE UNIFORMED POLICEMAN): Call the doctor, he's got to come right away... Wait for him outside, try not to create alarm in the building.
The officer goes out.

INSPECTOR DE VINCENZI (TO THE MAID): Did someone come to visit last night?

MAID: I don't know, Inspector, I stay on duty until I have served dinner, around nine o'clock, then I retire to my room, upstairs. I didn't hear anything and this morning...

She goes on crying.

INSPECTOR DE VINCENZI: Someone must have come, to create this disaster. Did the lady receive often?

MAID: Very rarely, Inspector.

Agent Cruni is back in the room, he too bends down next to the corpse.

INSPECTOR DE VINCENZI (TO THE MAID): Think about it calmly, miss... a woman... blond, or chestnut hair, who comes to the house... Anything come to mind?

MAID (HESITATES, REFLECTS): ...No... I don't think so...

AGENT CRUNI: And yet we have blond hair here, long... A woman without a doubt.

AGENT CRUNI (ADDRESSED TO INSPECTOR DE VINCENZI): Evidence!

INSPECTOR DE VINCENZI (GETTING UP): Uh, evidence, Cruni... The evidence... It makes everything so easy, doesn't it?

"Cut!"

Manlio Parrini has shouted his command and now gets up from his chair. He turns to a boy behind him.

"Let's look at it," he says. Ferdinando Scotti approaches him and says something softly, Sara De Viesti takes a few notes on her papers.

Then Parrini speaks again.

"Okay, we're almost there, let's do it again."

Then he gets up and turns to Cosimo Ardenzi, Inspector De Vincenzi, says something softly, some suggestion, clearly, because the other nods.

Everyone gets into position as before. The woman with the clapperboard leans toward a camera:

"De Angelis, four ten!"

"Quiet . . . Camera . . . Action!"